Total-E-Bound Publishing books
by Jaime Samms:

Tales from Rainbow Alley
Hotwired Heart

Anthologies
Saddle Up 'N Ride: Sing For Your Supper

I0542147

Tales from Rainbow Alley

FINDERS KEEPERS

JAIME SAMMS

Finders Keepers
ISBN # 978-0-85715-425-5
©Copyright Jaime Samms 2011
Cover Art by Lyn Taylor ©Copyright 2011
Interior text design by Claire Siemaszkiewicz
Total-E-Bound Publishing

FINDERS
KEEPERS

Dedication

My Word War Buddies, without whom, this first novel might never have happened. Hugs and my heartfelt thanks to you all for your support, Ladies.

Chapter One

Rory

The last lash fell. The searing pain had turned to buzzing numbness some time ago, and I congratulated myself on making it to the end, on counting every single lash in a loud enough voice to be heard. Kane wouldn't have anything to complain about tonight. At the last second, I remembered and kept my head down. Kane would let me know when—*if*—I could look up. I waited, my heart thudding, my entire rib cage shaking, and a pounding going through my head until it throbbed. I'd never been good at waiting.

The clop of my Dom's boots circled around from behind me, sounding loud over the dull thump of music from the club outside the door. The first thing to enter my view was the toe of one boot, then the butt of the short lash Kane had been using. He now used it to raise my chin.

"You can count," he said.

"It's what you asked—"

A sharp crack of the hard wooden handle on the underside of my chin clacked my teeth together. Bright pain from clipping my tongue sparked white spots and elicited a gasp. It effectively stopped the protest I should have known to keep to myself. Another bruise to add to my collection, but at least he didn't discipline further.

"Did I say you could speak?"

I stared up at him, mouth clamped shut.

He hit me again, a little harder. "Answer."

"No, Sir."

"That's right."

The lash butt lifted my chin higher, dragging me up to the limit of my reach. The hard butt dug into my jaw. My back screamed at the stretch on hot skin, and my already shaky legs threatened to cramp.

"Stay." He said it with about as much expression as he might have said it to a dog.

I stayed. Then I whimpered as the only support deserted me. Kane trailed the wooden handle down across my collarbone, sternum and belly, finally using it to lift my limp cock.

"What's this?"

I closed my eyes in defeat. The new bruise under my chin, the searing heat of the lash marks across my back, the agony of stiff muscles and now that torture instrument so near my delicate bits sent me into a tailspin of panic. I shuffled backward, knees scraping across the rubber mat, thigh and butt muscles screaming pain up my spine. I couldn't go far. The manacles around my wrists, holding my arms spread-eagled above my head, stopped me. New pain lanced down my arms to connect with all the other agonies and draw out another sharp gasp.

"Weak," Kane spat. My privates flopped against sweaty thighs as Kane retreated. "Why I bother with your training…"

I watched him as he backed away, tossed the crop on the table near the door, and pulled out a pack of smokes.

"Don't look at me, slave."

I dropped my gaze, then my head. If he couldn't see my face, he wouldn't see the tears. The rejection hurt more than the physical discomforts, and I knew that was pathetic. Still, ice sank through me, gripping my heart. What else did I have to do? I'd followed every instruction, tried to anticipate every wish and held back when I wanted to beg for surcease. Nothing I'd tried was enough to please this man. Four months, almost, and I had yet to earn a bare word of praise. He told me to try harder, to do better, and I would make it. Now, I wondered if I'd ever get any of it right.

Long minutes passed to the sound of Kane's puffing. The smell of smoke overpowered the stench of my own sweat. Finally, Kane shifted, clomped back over and released a lever that dropped my hands lower. I had enough slack now to sink back on my heels, relieve some of the strain on my legs and back. I didn't dare move, didn't risk disappointing my teacher further.

"I'm going to get a drink."

Still not a word of acknowledgement. It didn't matter. I'd stay, I'd wait. I'd be here like this when he got back, and maybe, just maybe, he'd be pleased enough to say something.

Briefly, the flashing light and din of the bar beyond our private room entered the dim space as Kane opened the door to let himself out. It faded again as the door swung shut. Still, I didn't dare relieve the strain, didn't dare rest. Kane could walk in any minute, and I would prove I was strong, and not the weakling he accused me of being.

I would.

I tried not to think how it might have been easier if I'd dared eat more at dinner, but that was a wasted thought. The lashing would have been worse if he thought I'd eaten too much, and not just across my back. I resisted glancing down at my concave stomach. I knew it was free of marks beyond a few old, fading bruises. That punishment hadn't been administered in over a week, at least. I'd figured that one out. If it was the only part of me that didn't have bruises and lines of punishment, at least it was something. It could only be a step in the right direction.

I hoped.

Time stretched, faded, disappeared into the fog of pain and stiffening muscles. The shameful tears dried on my cheeks, sweat dried on my thighs and calves and made them itch. It trickled down my back, burning as it went, telling me he'd opened the skin at least in a few places. It slid between my butt cheeks, slick and uncomfortable. The shivering overtook me so gradually, I didn't even notice until the restraints began to jangle.

I'd slumped by then, only the cuffs holding me up. Every muscle ached. When the draught from the open door blew across my frigid body, I couldn't even lift my head, never mind rise to my former kneeling position. The shivering turned convulsive, jerking at my arms and shooting pain from wrists to biceps. A garbled whimper that didn't even sound like me bubbled up and escaped.

"Mark!"

The shout knifed through my head. *Wrong.* Wrong name, wrong voice, wrong gender, even.

"Mark! Hurry!" The clack of high heels came at me from the doorway and I cringed, though physically, I was beyond moving.

Running steps approached from outside the room, and I struggled through the fog to present myself—what was left of me—with some sort of pride. It wouldn't last. It never did when Kane introduced strangers into our play. I strained to pull myself upright and to keep from crying out. I might not like it, but I didn't have a choice, and acceptance was preferable to protest. Another lesson I'd learned the hard way.

"Don't." A male voice, this time, but not Kane's. "Don't try to move just yet. I'm going to lower your arms. One at a time. Gina. Get something…"

"Yeah."

Hard heels clacked away, and I felt the right cuff release from my wrist. I didn't feel any actual contact, but I didn't have the strength to hold the arm up. There was only a throbbing ache as I tried to control it and couldn't. I didn't have a clue what to do. Was Kane just watching? Would he approve of my release? Would he just let it happen and punish me for it later?

I wanted to look up, to ask him, or read some clue as to what was going on his face. But I didn't dare. He hadn't given me permission, and I likely wouldn't be able to tell what he was thinking through all the makeup and theatrics anyway.

"Slowly." The man who'd released me supported my arm, lowered it gently to my side as pins and needles slithered up and down. I wanted to curl around it, cradle it, but I held in the gulps that were coming too near to being sobs as my fingers went from numb to icy, to flaming.

I was too terrified to do anything.

"I know. Shhh." A hand caressed my head. "It's okay."

Before I could even process what 'okay' might mean, something stiff and scratchy dropped over my shoulders and I flinched.

Weakness. Kane would respond to that. But it hurt. My back was on fire with pain, and that sensation only intensified with the weight of material rubbing on the tender wounds.

"A table cloth, Gina?"

"Shit, I couldn't find anything else."

"Go up to the office. Rolly has clothes up there. Tell him what's happened."

Office? I tried hard to focus. They wanted to tell people about this?

"No!" I managed to croak the word out. "Kane. Please."

I finally looked up, and there was no Kane. The bar beyond the propped-open door was dark and silent. In the room with me was a slim, dark-haired man with warm brown eyes watching me with concern, and a woman I recognised from behind the bar. Her colour-striped hair fell in long strands around her face, having escaped from her ponytail. She crossed her arms over her chest and blew at an offending rainbow-coloured lock.

There was no sign of Kane. I had no idea where he might have disappeared to.

"Where's — ?"

"Don't know," she barked.

Her light eyes snapped with anger, and I dropped my gaze.

"Sorry."

"Not your fault," the man assured me, once more caressing my hair. "Gina? Go get Rolly."

"No," I said. It came out a little steadier this time. This was humiliating enough. I didn't want anyone else involved.

"Gina, go." Mark's voice was gentle but firm. "He's the owner, sir." He touched my shoulder now, fingers featherlight against my skin. "I have to tell him. I'm sorry."

I nearly laughed at him calling me sir.

He moved slightly. I watched the shift of his jeans-clad knees. "Other arm now. You ready?"

I nodded, though the painful tingling hadn't yet left my other arm. It wasn't like I had a choice. I needed his help.

My left arm dropped into Mark's waiting hand, and he carefully lowered it. He took his time, but nothing could stop the pain of blood flowing back into the limb. I sucked breath through my teeth, groaned it out again, less concerned now about appearances. Kane wasn't here to impress, and it fucking hurt.

"I know. I'm sorry." That hand caressed my head again. "You're doing good...what's your name?"

"Rory. Rory Sanders."

"Good. Just try and relax, Rory. It'll pass."

It was plain Kane wasn't coming back. I curled around my throbbing arms and shook, telling myself I wasn't reacting to the small words of praise or the kind touch, telling myself I didn't ache inside because it wasn't Kane saying it, wasn't Kane there taking me down and comforting me. He'd hurt me, and he obviously didn't give a shit. That shouldn't hurt more than the physical side, but it did.

The starched cloth scraped at my tender skin, calling me back from the misery to attend to the very real demands of my abused body. My thigh and butt muscles cramped and complained. In the periphery of it all, Gina's heels clicked and clacked, returning to the room.

"Rolly told me to take a look," she said.

"Sure. Good idea." Mark leaned over me again. "Gina has EMT training, Rory. Let's let her have a look at your back and see if you need a doctor, okay?"

I nodded. This wasn't the worst whipping I'd received. It was the long hours bound uncomfortably and the humiliation, more than the lashing, that kept my head down and eyes averted as she came over and turned a light on my wounds.

I heard the small noise she made, the sharp intake of Mark's breath. No doubt the old bruises stood out in that bright glare, but in the end, she merely grunted, handed Mark a tube of something, and instructed him to rub it over the worst marks.

"It'll take the swelling down and help with the pain," she assured me. "No need to see a doctor."

Bless her. That would have been the ultimate devastation, to explain how this had happened.

Her heels clacked out again, and Mark and I were left alone. I stayed in my curled position, using the excuse of Mark rubbing the ointment into my back to stay huddled in on myself. He didn't speak as he worked, but his hands were gentle, and when he was done, despite the pain of his careful touch, I did feel better for the plain, compassionate attention.

"Can you stand?" His voice was about the only thing that didn't grate, and I nodded. "Gina brought you some clothes. Do you need help?"

"No!" I'd be damned if I'd let him dress me, too, no matter how nice he was being about it all.

"Okay." Mark's hand slipped under my elbow anyway, and he took my weight without comment as I struggled to get my feet under me. "Take your time. There's no hurry."

Ashamed by my weakness, I found I had to lean on him to stand. My legs were numb from being folded under me, and my knees protested at straightening. "Shit…" A string of swears followed as blood pounded through my body, a freight train of discomfort and pain to every extremity. Mark stood patiently, accepting my weight while the feeling came back to my feet. Finally, I straightened slightly, mustering enough motor control and presence of mind to take the clothing.

"I can manage." I pulled my elbow free of Mark's grasp and transferred my balance to the support beam of the room's restraint structure.

If he thought I was being ungrateful, he didn't show it. Instead, he nodded and backed up a step. "Okay."

Without a backward glance, he left me alone in the room. It took a good long while to fumble the borrowed sweats onto my body. My fingers felt fat as sausages, numb, and I had to sit to get my feet into the pants. By the time I made it to the door and opened it, enough time had passed to allow a little group to gather at the bar. Coffee cups with coffee that no longer steamed sat before them. They didn't talk, and only one of them looked up when I came out.

Mark and Gina sat at the bar, their backs to me. Another man—tall, blond and impossibly elegant in jeans and what should have been a ridiculous pirate shirt—leaned against the slick black expanse of countertop. He must be the owner. He had a proprietary air about him and his eyes glittered as I met his gaze.

Squaring my shoulders and steeling myself for their looks, I opened the door fully and tried not to shuffle as I made my way into the bar proper.

The blond pushed gracefully to his feet and peered at me. "How long were you in there?"

"Uh..." I frowned at the floor and found it odd that the dark hard wood wasn't scuffed or sticky. The place didn't behave much like a bar ought to. It was clean and smelled like the lemon freshener my mother's housecleaner had used on our kitchen floors. The bar sparkled under bright spotlights, and the booths to the sides huddled in their shadows, curtained interiors opened now to the rest of the room, their pendant lights dark and tables bare. The tall stools around the periphery perched, upturned like a flock of confused cranes, legs in the air, on the tables and counters.

I focused back on the question and tried to think. Time hadn't really registered. I knew we'd arrived at the bar shortly after midnight, I'd signed Kane in as my guest at twelve-thirteen according the electronic ID monitor, and now that quick glance around told me the place was closed and had been for some time. That meant it was at least after three, probably closer to four. How much of the intervening time I'd actually spent with Kane, and how much alone, I had no idea.

"'Uh'...?" the blond prompted. His brow furrowed. "Okay, then. You didn't arrive here naked." He lowered his chin and peered at me, exactly like a reprimanding father. I only just stopped myself stepping back from that thought. That look had never lasted long on my own father's face before the cuffing had begun. "Someone would have noticed," he pointed out, his voice heavy with sarcasm, an emotion I recognised, and I bit my lip to keep it from trembling. "So where are your clothes?"

"Rolly." Mark rose and stepped forward, but a sharp look from Rolly stopped him cold. His head dropped, and he backed up a step.

I got the distinct impression Mark had just been slapped down, and I looked again at the blond. He had an imperious air about him, and his gaze was hard. Like Kane's. He glared at Mark like he owned him.

The look gave me the shivers, and I stepped up, drawing his attention away, wishing I hadn't done or said whatever I had that had been wrong. I didn't want Mark getting in trouble because of me. "I...I'm sorry, I don't know."

"You came alone?"

"N-no."

"Who with?"

"Well. That is, I arrived alone. I met Kane here, outside, and signed him in."

"Where's your ID bracelet?" Bright eyes I could now see were disconcertingly green flashed to my bare wrists and back to my face.

"With my clothes? I had to take it off for...for the cuffs." I rubbed at the residual sensation on my wrists, as if anyone here didn't know what I was talking about. That I'd lost the ID bracelet was bad. Access to this club was a rare and exclusive commodity. I'd paid through the nose and filled out endless forms, accepted numerous security checks. Likely, once escorted out, I would not be allowed back. Another strike against me for Kane to punish. He'd been adamant that I find a way to get us in here. Another of his tests I'd failed. I hoped against hope he had the ID tag.

"That's it?" Rolly asked when I fell silent and didn't elaborate.

"Rolly!" This time, Mark ignored the sharp look the blond shot him and stepped forward. "Take it easy. This is not his doing."

"This is my place, Mark." Rolly's fists balled, but Mark didn't flinch or back down.

"I know." Mark placed a hand on one of Rolly's wrists. The fist there slowly uncurled, though the look of fierce anger Rolly turned on Mark didn't soften. "I know how serious this is, but take it easy on him. He didn't do anything wrong."

For a long minute, the two men stared at one another. There was no mistaking the power dynamic there, or that Mark was severely overstepping some invisible but very real boundary.

A sudden shiver ripped through me, convulsing my shoulders. It was the exact same haughty look in Rolly's eyes when he looked at Mark as I'd so often received from Kane.

Mark straightened his shoulders and retrieved his hand, but he didn't look away or back down.

"Please don't..." I stepped forward, and both men turned to look at me. I shrank from Rolly's hard gaze, but what else could happen to me tonight? It wouldn't be fair for Mark to take a punishment meant for me. "Please. This was my fault. Don't get mad at him."

"Shit." Rolly's inflexible stance relaxed, and he rolled his eyes. "This was not your fault." He passed a hand over his face. "I'm sorry." Firm fingers wrapped over Mark's shoulder, he sighed and gave him a quick peck on his cheek before turning back to me with a taut, forced calm. "You did nothing wrong. I'll make sure you get a replacement tag." His attention shifted briefly to Mark. "Call Gabe—make a copy of the security tapes, though I'm sure we won't find anything this time, either. And make up signage. No more makeup, ID tag or not. Not until this freak is found and stopped. No one hides behind a fake face in here."

Mark nodded. "Yes, sir."

Rolly's focus settled back on me. "You aren't the first one we've found left alone like that. I was hoping...no one seems to really *know* this guy."

"What?" The bar tilted, and I reached for a nearby stool. "He's...I thought..."

"Geez, Rolly." Mark pushed past his lover and reached for me, easing me into a comfortable chair. "Here. Sit. Gina, get him something to drink."

"I thought we were... He..." I swallowed a lump of bile and lowered my head to my arms on the bar. "I'm an idiot."

A steaming mug of coffee appeared at my elbow a second later. I lifted my head and stared into the black depths, unable to look any of the well-meaning strangers in the eye. "He never told me there was anyone else," I said dully. "I was stupid to think I was the only one."

Stupid to think I ever mattered at all.

"This is not your fault," Mark said firmly, pushing my cup a little closer and encouraging me to pick it up. "Know that right now. He's pathological."

"That the strongest you got?" I asked, still watching the bubbles on top of the coffee pop, one by one.

"Here." Gina picked up the mug and took me gently by the elbow, pulling me off the bar stool. "Come sit down over here." In the periphery of my vision, I saw her jerk her head at her companions, indicating they should back off. It shamed me to admit it, even to myself, but it was more comfortable to be alone in the tight booth with her, than to have the two men, however well-meaning, hovering over me.

She smiled and patted my shoulder. "Boss's orders about the coffee. Sorry."

I just looked at her blankly.

"In case this Kane asshole...gave you anything."

"Drugs?" I shook my head. "No. I don't do drugs."

"You might not know if he had."

"Fuck." I dropped my head into my hands. This just got better and better. "I'm an idiot."

"No." Her hand landed on my forearm, and she rubbed lightly up and down. "No. You're not."

Nice of her to say, but I'd put myself in the hands of a man who didn't give a shit about me, and worse, who apparently actively set out to hurt people. He could have killed me, and I'd blithely trusted him because he told me to. It didn't get dumber than that.

"Honey, just let the boss call the shots for now. He really does want to help. He's just...gruff sometimes." Once again, she pushed the still-steaming mug forward. "Drink."

I glanced over to where Rolly leaned against the bar watching me. "He the boss of everyone?"

"Around here?" Gina shrugged and let out a small chuckle. "Pretty much. But don't let him scare you. He really is a good guy. A little stressed lately, but good at heart."

"He owns the club?"

"Yeah." Gina slipped into the booth across from me. "And Marky." She smiled, a soft, almost devoted expression. "They're very good for each other."

"Him and Mark?"

"Yeah."

I studied them. Rolly was looking over Mark's head, watching our booth, his pale eyes glittering from under long bangs. It felt like he was peeling away my skin and bone, seeing right inside me to the ache that had begun when I first met Kane face to face—and had grown to consume everything since. Mark stood in front of Rolly—his back to the booth so I couldn't see his face, or hear what he was saying—but after a minute, Rolly's focus switched from me to Mark.

Cupping one hand around the back of Mark's head, Rolly pulled him into a kiss that had my cock twitching. Mark melted, leaning in, and when his hands came up to grip the front of Rolly's shirt, that's when I noticed the cuffs on both his wrists, well-worn and comfortable-looking.

Mark's groan carried across the intervening space, and Rolly tightened his hand on the back of his neck.

"You will not," Rolly said, "even consider any such thing. You belong to me. There will not be further talk about making yourself bait, even in theory. No."

Mark nodded, and his own fingers tightened, gripping Rolly's shirt in his fists. "It was just an idea."

"No." Rolly kissed him again, and Mark's moan carried, his stance shifted, and when Rolly abruptly ended the kiss, just as Mark was reaching for more, it was clear Mark had been chastised. He kept his gaze down and stood placidly under Rolly's hand, still on his neck in a possessive grip. Rolly met my gaze again, troubled, but determined.

"Go upstairs, Mark. Call Gabe."

Mark nodded and moved instantly to follow Rolly's orders, not in the least fazed by having been publicly told his place.

Had I really thought Kane could give me that? I turned reluctantly back to Gina. Maybe if I kept talking, I wouldn't have to think. "You work here long?"

"Going on three years."

"Really? Low turnover."

"I told you. Rolly's good people. Good boss. I tend bar, but that's not why he hired me. I was an EMT. I had a few…issues with the way the system treated me and my girlfriend, the way it treats most openly gay people.

Rolly hired me to keep his staff healthy. He's paying my way through school. I'll be an NP when I'm done, and he'll pay me what I'm worth, and treat me like a person.

"'Most everyone on staff isn't just a waiter or a bartender. Rolly hires good people, keeps us trained, and lets us use our skills. He'll say he does it to keep his empire intact, but if he was only about the money and the power, Rainbow Alley wouldn't be the place it is. He uses what he has to keep this neighbourhood safe. People say he's dangerous, but I think that's only if you do something to piss him off or hurt him. He has a very long reach and a very extended group of people under his umbrella of protection. That's why he's so pissed about Kane. He's going to come down on that bastard, and I don't want to see what's left."

She reached over, hesitated, and I consciously made the effort not to pull back. She placed a hand lightly over my wrist. "What happened?"

So much for not thinking about it. I considered the question for a moment and realised I didn't have an answer. "I don't know," I said at last, the words drifting quietly across the space between us. "I screwed up. I thought…"

"Thought what?" she prompted.

"I did what he asked. I did."

"But?" Her questions should have felt invasive, but her voice and demeanour were too gentle to set me on edge.

"It hurt."

"You didn't ask him to stop?"

"I thought…" I went back, trying to figure out what I *had* been thinking. "I thought pleasing him was more important than an erection." Heat flashed through me, leaving behind clammy sweat and embarrassment at the confession, but she didn't say anything. "He didn't think so. He said he was going for a drink. He never came back."

"So…" She frowned, picked at a tiny bit of bubbled lacquer on the table top. Her glance, when she raised her lashes, was quick and penetrating. "He chastised you for not getting hard when he hurt you?"

When she put it like that, it sounded just what it was—weak and stupid—and my cheeks flamed hot. "It made more sense in the moment," I lied, wanting that to be true and knowing it wasn't.

"Lots of things do," she agreed mildly. "Walk me through it."

"What?"

"Whose idea was it to come here? Why here? Why not at home?"

"Uh." I picked up my mug at last, a woefully inadequate bit of ceramic to hide behind, but I needed to collect my thoughts.

She merely waited, pushed a few crumbs around the table top, and watched me.

"His idea. There is no 'home'. I mean…I have a home. He's never been, and I don't know where he lives. We've always used clubs. He wanted to come here especially, though. He didn't really say why—I suppose because it's exclusive and posh."

"It is that. What about hotels? Ever use a hotel?"

"At first. Before it got really serious, but he was never very…comfortable. I got the feeling he doesn't like hotels."

"Of course not. Too conspicuous, and possibly traceable," she muttered.

"He wasn't hiding anything." Except how could I really believe that when, if pressed, I wouldn't be able to accurately describe the man? He'd refused to get the club membership here, even though it would have been far easier for him, and he'd signed only 'Kane' at the door. He always wore a pancake of gothic makeup, and his hair colour changed with his whims. I'd be useless to a police sketch artist, and the thought that this conversation might end with that very eventuality set me shivering all over again.

"So, his not having anything to hide is why he closed you in a dark room and locked the door when he left?"

"He what?" When I looked at her, she just met my gaze with a straight, bland stare. "Locked the door?"

She nodded. "And took the key with him so no one would open that door until I used the master key to go in and clean. He didn't want you found too soon."

"I don't understand."

"Neither do we." The deeper voice dropped from above, and I looked up into Mark's fine features. "Rory, this is Gabriel Stark. He'd like to ask you a few questions."

"Why?" I glanced over to the taller, broad man standing beside Mark.

Pale grey eyes, anything but faded, watched me, their steady light turning my insides to something hot and liquid. It was a moment of heart-thudding distraction before I noticed his square hand stretched out to shake. I placed my hand in his dry, calloused one, and sure as shit he felt me shake as his fingers closed over mine, not in a crushing grip, but in a firm, reassuring hold that completely swallowed my smaller hand.

Gabriel's strong jaw twitched once and went still. When I met his gaze, his eyes widened slightly, his fingers tightening.

Nerves jangled through me. I pushed a flop of thick curls out of my face and lifted my chin, but when his brows came down, fine and sharp, I looked away first. It didn't stop my heart from pounding or prompt me to let go until he did, though. Somehow, there was comfort in that grip, and it wasn't just because he could have walked out of my favourite wet dream. Chances of him being the Dom I'd been looking for all along were slim, and even if he did play that way, once he found out what a fool I was, he'd want nothing more to do with me.

"So." I sucked in a breath, like it was going to fortify me somehow, and managed to meet his eye again. "Who are you?"

"That depends," he said carefully. "Right now, I'm a friend of Rolly's, and a friend of yours, I hope."

I said nothing. What was there to say?

"We have to get to the bottom of this, Rory," Rolly interjected, "and you, frankly, are the best chance we've had. Some of the other victims this *Kane* person," he spat the name as though it tasted foul, "left us were so drugged and out of it, they barely knew their own names, let alone what had happened to them."

"I'm not a victim," I said quickly. "I came here on my own. He asked–"

"We know." Mark shifted to put himself between me and his partner. "Gabe here is an expert. He's going to help you."

"I don't need help." I got laboriously to my feet and shuffled as quickly towards the front of the club as my stiffening muscles allowed. "I'm fine. I'm going home. I'm sorry about your problem, but I can't tell you anything else."

"You going out into the street in bare feet?" Gabriel's voice rumbled low through the still room, vibrating through my gut and loosening all the carefully held together bits. Goose bumps crawled slippery fingers up my arms. That voice, velvety smooth over steel, stopped me in place. "Sit down."

The command in his voice was like warmed chocolate pouring down my spine.

I found myself turning and retaking my seat before I'd even thought about it.

"Good."

My cheeks heated, but I couldn't find my indignation under the relief of having just done the first right thing all night.

"Gina," Gabe stepped past Mark and touched her shoulder, "a cup for me too, please?"

"Sure thing, Gabby."

Gabe's low rumble settled in my gut, gluing some of those bits back together, but Gina's grey eyes crinkled as her face softened into a smile, and suddenly, there was an unmistakable family resemblance.

"Honestly," Gabe muttered as he took her seat across from me. "Some nicknames just stick with you in the worst way, don't they?"

I watched him, nodded, and kept watching. It confused me a little how Gabe's microscopic scrutiny of my face didn't put me on edge. If Kane looked at me like that, I'd have bypassed edgy right into panic over trying to figure out what I'd done wrong to warrant it. Gabe just took in everything he saw without comment until Gina returned with his coffee.

Finally, he looked away. "Thanks, sis. Do me a favour. Go over every inch of that room—"

"I know what to look for." For the first time, her voice took on a bit of the same hard edge as Rolly's had. "If there's anything there, I'll find it."

Gabe nodded his thanks. She squeezed his muscled biceps and left the table.

"You two can go." Gabe waved a hand, shooing Mark and Rolly off. "Do whatever. I got this."

"You got what, exactly?" I flinched at the husky grate of my own voice and the way it broke over my uncertainty. The sharp edges could shred everything that came out of me. I took my hands from where they had fastened tightly around my mug and rubbed them on my thighs under the table. They trembled anyway, as I shoved hair out of my face.

"There are people in the world you need to be afraid of," Gabe said, picking up his own mug. "I will never be one of them, I can assure you of that." He sipped, eyes fixed on my face again, his free hand relaxed on the tabletop.

"Who are you, exactly?" I asked, consciously placing my own hands back on the cool, smooth surface.

"Gabriel Stark."

"Yeah. Mark said…"

"Other than that, it depends on the day. I trained most of the submissives who work for Rolly." He gave a negligent little tip of his head to one side. "On my days off, I'm a private investigator."

"Why…" I swallowed a few times and found myself scrubbing my palms back and forth over the soft fleece of my pants again. "Why did they call you?"

"Because I go where cops don't, investigate what they can't…or won't."

I nodded, immediately seeing how this would qualify.

"So Kane," I took a deep breath, "he's done…" I floundered. I didn't know how to phrase it.

"Some reprehensible things, and I mean to stop him. Will you help me?"

That was unexpected. "Help you?"

Gabe merely nodded—a curt dip of his chin—took another sip of his coffee, and pulled out a pad of paper and a pen.

"I don't understand. They said you were here to help me."

Gabe set his pen down neatly beside his notebook. "We can help each other." He moved his coffee mug to one side, moved mine beside it, and leant forward on his elbows over the table. "First, I need to know everything you and Kane have done together."

"That's private!" My hopes plummeted. He'd played me, trying to get me to trust him. "None of your fucking business."

Gabe didn't flinch from the outburst. "This is going to be difficult for you, Rory. Beyond difficult. You probably think, right now, that what I'm asking is impossible. I don't blame you for thinking that."

"Y-you want me to tell you about my sex life."

Gabe studied me closely for a long minute, until I once again found the reflective black surface of the table between us fascinating. The glossy surface fogged under my sweaty palms, and I curled my fingers into fists to hide their trembling.

"Why?" I asked, finally, voice barely above a whisper. "Why do I have to tell you those things?"

"Because if I'm going to stop him doing this to others, I need to know just exactly what it is he's done to you. Knowing what he's done will help me to figure out why, and that will help me figure out what kind of man he is, who he is, and where I might find him."

"*With* me," I whispered, knowing how desperate it sounded. For some unfathomable reason, I wanted Gabe to believe me. But how could he, when I didn't really think it was truth myself anymore?

"*To* you, Rory." Gabe's big hand came down to cover my more delicate one. "You need to learn the difference."

I yanked free. "Is that how you're going to help me?" I jerked up out of my seat. "You going to show me? Take his place?" Anger and fear collided, smashing my insides to pulp between them. "I don't—I don't want—" I slid out of the booth, backed across the floor, shaking a hand in front of me, warding something off, though Gabe hadn't moved a muscle.

For the first time since they'd rescued me, I felt the dim lighting close in, the darkened bar fade to a cavern of menace and secrets. I trembled all over, wanting to go home, away from all of it, to forget I'd ever thought being submissive was something I should try. My back fetched against the cold, clear glass of the front door, but it didn't yield under the pressure of my pushing on it.

"I won't make you do anything you don't want, Rory. Lesson number one. You are in charge. Nothing happens without your consent."

"Then I don't want to talk about it. Any of it!" I closed my fingers over the smooth bar of the door handle, an anchor in the encroaching darkness.

"Will you grant me the answer to just one question, then?" Gabe asked. His gaze didn't waver as he picked up his mug and sipped.

"Depends on the question."

He placed the mug down again, and his lips tightened.

"A-are you angry?" I reinforced my grip on the door handle, clinging to the hard metal as my guts tingled and dissolved into a mess at my feet. My back stung with the sudden breakout of sweat over my skin. "I'll answer. Please, just ask so I can answer and go home." Terror dropped my voice back to a whisper. "Please."

"That is answer enough for what I was going to ask, Rory."

"I don't understand."

Gabe finally got up and walked slowly across the floor, approaching like I was a cornered dog. His hands remained loose at his sides, and he stopped when he reached the end of the bar—a nice, non-threatening distance. "The question was, do you enjoy it?"

I frowned. "Enjoy it? He—" I thought back to the small, bare room, the rubber flooring, the racks and the way my shoulders had ached. My hands still felt fat and clumsy from the hours of poor circulation. I remembered asking why we had to do something so personal in a public place. Why not in private, something between the two of us? Given the way things had turned out, I should be glad it had been here. What would have happened to me if Kane had left me like that in my house, a place I rarely shared with anyone? How long would I have been bound, alone, before someone found me?

A convulsive shudder rocked me, and a sound very like a whimper escaped before I could stop it. "How is that enjoyable? How does anyone enjoy that?" I didn't want to sob the words out. I couldn't stop my throat closing over them, couldn't stop the need to squeeze them out, to ask the question. How did Kane take so much pleasure in my pain?

"I can answer that."

I whipped my head up to look past Gabe to the steps leading up to the club's office. Mark stood there, looking down on us, his hands gripping the stair rail. The buckles on his cuffs glinted as he came slowly down the steps.

"The first time Rolly put these on me," he held up one hand to show off his cuff, "I was terrified. I didn't know him. He plucked me out of a nightmare, brought me to his home. He could have kept me there, prisoner, forever. He didn't. He let me say no. I didn't, but he gave me the option. No one had ever given me the option before that night. I never felt safer than that, than I have ever since. He never lets me down. He's there when I need him, he trusts me, and I trust him. And, he taught me to trust myself. I owe him everything. I enjoy serving him.

"I grew up on the streets, Rory. No one ever telling me how to live, how to behave. I was my own master. At least, that's what I thought. I was wrong, of course, because you don't own even yourself in a gang. But I didn't realise until Rolly released me from all that just how wrong I was. I didn't even know how trapped I was in that life until he took me out of it and brought me into his. I'd never had a choice about anything until Rolly came along."

"That hardly sounds like it has anything at all to do with…with sex. Kane's…different."

"It has *nothing* to do with sex. It has to do with love and trust and communication. Sex is something else entirely. I came to Rolly's domination through sex because that's what I understood at the time. It's grown into my life, I've grown to understand who I am, and now sex is just a highly pleasurable manifestation of what I feel for him. Kane…" He didn't finish, but his soft brown eyes took on a glint that made his streetwise past come alive and deadly on his face.

I looked from Mark to Gabe. "But you train submissives."

"I do. Sexually and otherwise. For Rolly, I train them to be sexual submissives. Some of them want more, and I help them find what they're looking for, if I can."

Mark had come the rest of the way down the stairs and across the dark bar. Now he reached over and touched my wrist with two fingers, gaining my attention. "Let him help you, Rory. He knows what he's doing. He can teach you—"

"What makes any of you think I want anything to do with this, ever again?" I rattled the door handle, frantic, feeling the room and the presence of too many people watching close in.

"If nothing else," Gabe said quietly, easing Mark away from me with a hand on his arm, "let me take you home, explain a few things. I'm not going to force you to do anything. You can call someone, if you want." He pulled a cell from his shirt pocket and handed it to me.

I shook my head, knowing there was no one I could call, but not wanting them to know that. I'd had a narrow escape and knew it. I didn't need to inform a whole raft of people I was essentially alone in the world, and at the moment, helpless, locked in with strangers. I had nothing except my gut instinct to tell me if any of them were any different from Kane. Fat lot of good my instinct had done so far.

"Call him a cab," Gina suggested.

"Does Kane know where you live?" Rolly asked from where he'd taken a seat at the far end of the bar.

I nodded, miserable. "He knows my address."

"Is it inside the Alley?"

"No."

"There's no one there to look out for you." This was not a question, and Rolly stood, pacing the bare dance floor, eyes troubled.

It was enough to grow new fear in my gut. What if Kane was there waiting for me? I raised pleading eyes to Mark. "Can I stay with you?"

Mark looked to Rolly, and I immediately knew the answer. Rolly's eyes glittered. However good he was, whatever he did for his community, some things he did not share. Access to Mark, to his personal space, were high on that list. I shrank back again, leaning on the door. "Never mind."

"You can come to mine," Gabe said at last.

I looked to Gina, but Rolly was already shaking his head. "No. I'm not risking her. Stay with Gabe for the rest of the night. He can take you home in the morning, check the place out. Make sure you're safe."

I wondered if I'd ever feel safe again. I lifted my gaze to meet Gabe's and sighed. His pale grey eyes were clear, open, his expression patient. He leaned on the end of the bar, hands perched on the edge behind him, just waiting, watching, saying nothing.

"Okay," I agreed at last, and let go of my death grip on the door handle.

"Chin up," Gabe said softly. "We'll get this figured out." He moved away from the bar, one small step in my direction. "You'll feel safe again, Rory. I promise you that. I'll make sure he never hurts you again."

I nodded, straightened, and moved so Mark could let us out. I don't know why I believed Gabe. Believed him like I had never managed to believe Kane, no matter how smooth-tongued the man had been. And when Gabe settled his hand on the small of my back to usher me out the door, I didn't flinch. Instead, a flutter of relief, and something else loosened some of the tension inside. Maybe it would be okay.

Gina produced a pair of flip-flops from somewhere and handed me the tube of ointment for my back.

"Thanks."

"Take care of yourself, Rory. And stay in touch, yeah?"

I nodded, unsure why she cared, but it was nice that she did.

The bar's door closed behind us with a soft *thwoop*, and Gabe pointed out his car, a nice, unassuming sedan next to the exit. He even opened the door for me. There was no denying I felt cared for, looked after. I wanted to believe it was about me. I couldn't, quite, but it was a nice fantasy for a few hours, and I let myself just accept it.

Chapter Two

Gabe

I watched him slink to the car, steps slow, head down. It was a shame, because all that glorious black hair, falling in waves just past his shoulders, was blocking my view of his delicate but decidedly masculine face. His skin was pale, and it was hard to tell if that was a result of his ordeal or if he was naturally milky white. His black eyes stood out against that paleness, and his lips, full and pouty, took on a sultry depth of colour. If Snow White had been a man, this was what he'd have looked like, and it set my blood on fire. He was thin, though. I could see it even under the baggy sweats. He carried himself like a frail, frightened puppy, kicked too often, and it stimulated my need to protect him.

I told myself it had nothing to do with his resemblance to a dead man I hadn't been able to help. That was coincidence. The resemblance was purely physical. Rory had something my lost lover never had. He had himself, still. He wasn't past the point of no return. Not yet.

I noted that he walked with his back held stiff. I would have to figure out a way to get that shirt off, to check the damage. Mark had said it didn't look bad, and I trusted my sister's assessment as well, but the way he was carrying himself told me it hurt. My worry was confirmed when he climbed into the car then curled forward so his back didn't touch the seat.

"Belt."

He nodded silently and fastened his seat belt, but still held himself away from the seat.

"I know you don't know me, Rory. You have no reason to trust me. It speaks well of you that you are cautious, in fact."

"But?"

"But nothing. I'm not going to hurt you. I'm not going to make you answer anything you don't want to."

Rory nodded, peering out the side window. His pale face was drawn into a tight frown, his dark eyes glimmered softly, and I itched to tuck the long black hair away from his cheek, to be able to see him better. I kept my hands on the wheel and reminded myself that however delicious he was, he was also broken, and I had no right to make his life harder. It killed me he would rather go home with a stranger, after what he'd just been through, than call a friend. No one should be that alone in the world.

"How much...what do you need to know to...stop him?"

The question surprised me, and I glanced at him again to see those big black eyes turned on me. I had to force calm I wasn't exactly feeling. He was too beautiful, even scared shitless, and I knew I was falling way too fast. I had to stay detached to do him any good.

"Well." I focused back on the road, made myself look away, and smoothed over the stuttering he was causing within my heart. He couldn't be allowed see it. It would only spook him more. "The more you can tell me, the more chance I have of figuring out who he is and why he's doing this."

"You said he'd done it before. To others."

I nodded. The creep was making the entire community antsy. Tension in the neighbourhood was rising steadily, and the sooner we stopped the guy, the better for everyone, not just hapless subs who fell under his dubious spell.

"Why?"

"I wish I knew, Rory. He's sick. Twisted." I shook my head, as confused about it as he was. "I don't know. I will figure it out, though. I promise you that."

I could still feel his huge, cavernous eyes on me. I didn't dare look at him, for fear of getting lost in them. I had to be very, very careful. I could totally destroy him if I wasn't, and I wanted him whole again.

And why, do you think? Be careful, Gabriel. You know it's a slippery slope…

A slope I'd started down the moment I laid eyes on him.

At my house, just a little, white clapboard affair on a quiet street in the centre of one of Rainbow Alley's little cul-de-sac neighbourhoods, I pulled the car into the garage and let us inside. He stopped on the kitchen threshold and looked around.

"Nice." A full chorus of appreciation in one word. "You cook a lot."

I smiled. That he could see that about me just by looking at my kitchen was a good sign. If the world was starting to make that amount of sense to him, he was finding his way out of the shock on his own.

"I do. You?"

He nodded, shuffling over to the stove and running his fingers lightly along the edge. "Yeah. Been on my own a long time. No one's going to do it for me. Don't have gas, though. This is a nice range." He opened the oven door, bent to look inside, unable to hide the wince as his shirt stretched across his back. "Convection." He closed it again, straightened, and a delicate pink spread over his cheeks. "God. I'm sorry. I—"

"It's fine." I let the smile settle into my features. Maybe he wasn't as desperately broken as I thought. "In fact, I could eat a little something. You?"

He stood still, watching me, his hands twisted together in front of him, like he was considering something, then he nodded. "Can I make you something?"

My eyebrows shot up. I couldn't hide the expression, and tried to soften it with a wider smile. He was adorable, eager. No wonder that Kane asshole had treated him so much worse than the others. Rory *wanted* to serve. He wanted to please, and he didn't even realise how natural the desire was. Kane would have taken complete advantage of that, pushing and pushing until Rory shattered. I hoped to hell he hadn't got that far yet, that I could fix what was broken and help him find himself again.

"Yes, Rory, that would be perfect." I pulled out a kitchen chair and sat down. "Anything you need, just ask."

I couldn't have asked for a more perfect set-up. He was completely at home in the kitchen, at ease, probably like he wouldn't be under most other circumstances. I could see the tension melting out of him as he worked, digging through the fridge for sandwich ingredients and opening and closing the cupboards, looking for plates and glasses.

He made BLT's. Easy, simple, but mixing herbs into the mayo, making the snack into something special. He smiled, pleased, when he found my assortment of beer, chose a couple of light lagers, and placed them on the counter beside the glasses.

"I found Kane online." His quiet voice carried in the small kitchen, but he focused all his attention on spreading mayo over toast, as though the tiniest misstep would ruin his master work. "I was…exploring. I thought it would be good to read up. Join some groups." He glanced over at me, a small smile flitting across his face, looking for reassurance, maybe.

I nodded. "It is good to get all the information you can."

"You never know, though, do you? Who you're really talking to? I thought, well, I didn't know what I was doing. He seemed nice. He answered all my questions." His brow furrowed. "I trusted him. Stupid, I guess."

Yes, stupid. But understandable. For someone looking for answers in the confusing world of the lifestyle, it was never easy to figure out who was telling you the truth, who was telling you what they wanted you to believe, and who was just talking out their ass.

"If you can remember any of the sites you visited, any other people you talked to, it might help us locate him."

Rory nodded, bit his lower lip as he carefully sliced through the tomato, and I had to refocus my attention from his face to his hands as my heart rate shot up. He was going to kill me without ever knowing he had an effect. My heart would explode.

"We can pick up my laptop tomorrow, maybe. I have bookmarks."

"Good idea." I smiled as he glanced over, and was rewarded with a bright, if fleeting, grin.

He had the bacon sizzling and was slicing the cheese before he spoke again. "He said if I did everything he asked, if I pleased him, he'd…" A deeper blush stained his cheeks, and he shook his head, causing the shaggy hair to tumble down and hide his face. "Not that I've never…before. I have. Just not… Well, anyway, I never got there, did I? I was never good enough."

I didn't quite know what Kane had promised him, but it didn't really matter. What mattered was the method, the lies he'd been fed.

"That's wrong." I did my best not to let my frustration show.

"Huh?" His eyes flashed bright as his head snapped up. "What's wrong?"

"Did he ever ask you what you liked? What you wanted?"

"Sure. That's what he said we'd do if I gave him what he wanted."

"That isn't how it works, Rory."

Delicate furrows creased his brow. "What do you mean? It's my job to please him—"

"And his to look after you. He didn't do that. No." I leaned onto the table, clasping my hands in front of me, studying my fingers as I tried to explain, to yet another sub, how the game was supposed to go. "Before he ever touched you, he should have asked you what you wanted, and more importantly, what you didn't want. He should have found your limits and never crossed them."

"How did I know what my limits were? What they are? I've never done this before. He said he'd help me find them."

I caught his eye, and his hands stilled, slices of cheese crumbling between his fingers. "Under the guise of doing whatever he wanted and telling you to be patient, that you would grow to like it. That if you just got through it for him, he'd reward you."

Rory didn't speak, didn't confirm or deny my supposition, but the pallor of his cheeks and the state of the cheese, disintegrating in his curled fingers, was answer enough.

"I'm an idiot," he mumbled, eyes going dark, face crumbling like the cheese.

"No." I couldn't keep my seat and watch him fall apart. I got up and went to him, placing a hand on his shoulder. When he didn't pull away, I took the other shoulder, too, and turned him to face me. "No, Rory, you aren't. He's a predator. He took advantage of what you didn't know. He fed you lies."

"You must think I'm a complete fool."

Carefully, I lifted his face, hoping he wouldn't shrink back. "I think he's the fool, for not knowing how to treat a treasure like you. He had a chance at something wonderful, and he had no idea." They were words I'd spoken often, to subs needing just the kind of re-education Rory needed, but looking into his eyes, seeing the fear and uncertainty, seeing the need for a friend, for just one person to treat him well, I'd never meant them like I did now. And all that need, all his desire to be accepted went straight to my dick, made my head swim, brought me too dangerously close to making some stupid, inappropriate comment or gesture. He needed a friend now, not another Dom trying to get into his pants.

Then he sobbed. I knew it was coming. It had to, eventually. I'd expected him to hold it in until he was alone. Most did. Most would rather suffer alone through the humiliation than admit they were ashamed, terrified, or anything other than pissed off. He didn't. He flung himself against me, wrapped his arms around my middle, and I fell, headlong, landing at the bottom of that slope a mess of sticky emotions.

"It's okay." I touched his hair, listening to him choke back the sobs, and finally let myself hold him. It lasted only a second before he was wincing and pulling away.

"Sorry!" I'd forgotten about his back.

"It's okay." He blinked and rubbed at his face, smearing the tears cross his cheek as he turned away to flip the bacon in the pan.

"Rory, I know you probably don't like the idea, but it would be best if you let me look at your back. Just to be sure."

I knew Gina was plenty competent enough to know if he'd needed a doctor or not, and to get him one if he did. Rolly protected his business, his property, with the best people, myself included. While I didn't always agree with his methods, I had to admire his effectiveness. He hired the best, people who would follow his direction, but would also speak up and demand he listen to their advice. If Gina thought Rory needed medical attention, she would have insisted he get it immediately. I still wanted to know exactly what I was dealing with.

Rory sniffled, but to my surprise, he nodded. "After we eat, okay? After that. I'm...I'm hungry."

"Sure." I took my seat again and contented myself with watching him work. He cut more cheese, cleaned as he went, and it was with something like satisfaction that I could see him work himself back to a kind of equilibrium.

He ate only a few bites of his sandwich and drank only a sip or two of beer. I was reasonably sure Kane hadn't drugged him. I was beginning to understand a little bit about the guy from the victims he'd left behind. He drugged the more belligerent ones, but seemed to enjoy pushing his more pliant victims towards their limit without dulling their sensations or distancing the poor men from what was happening to them. Seeing just how accommodating Rory was, I knew Kane would have thought him a prize.

"This might be the best BLT I've ever had," I told him, not even stretching the truth. Whatever he'd added to the mayo made all the difference.

He smiled, a shy little turning up of his lips, and ducked his head.

"Don't look down." I couldn't help reaching and lifting his chin again. "I'm serious. It's very good. Thank you."

"You're welcome."

I didn't imagine his chest puff out a tiny bit, and he met my eye, his glowing with a faint bit of pride. The sight gave me hope again. He bounced between desperate and tough so fast it was hard to know where he would land, but I had hope for him.

When I was done, he offered to clean up, and I smiled but kept him at the table with me, gently touching his hand.

"Are you trying to put off showing me your back?"

He blushed again, and I had to bite my tongue. He was nothing if not very, very pretty when he did that. He nodded, but this time he didn't look away. "Sorry."

"Don't be. I understand, but it isn't just idle curiosity. I want to make sure you're okay. I want to look after you. Will you let me?"

He didn't look away when he nodded this time, either, and every instinct in me screamed at me to praise him for it.

"Good. Rory, this is good. Let's get these dishes to the sink, then I want you to go upstairs to the bathroom at the end of the hall. I'll meet you there."

"Okay." He seemed more relaxed, now, and when he set his dishes beside the sink, he turned, pinning me with his gaze. "Gabe…do you think…?"

I waited, but he didn't continue, and finally, I felt I had to reassure him. "At the club, you said you were done with all this, and that's fine. I respect that. Even if you don't change your mind about letting me teach you, you can still ask me anything. If I can, I'll answer, I promise."

"Am I weak? Because I couldn't do what he wanted? Was I supposed to be stronger?"

"I think you're strong, Rory, because you're facing this, letting people help. He wanted what wasn't his to ask for."

"What do you ask for, Gabe? When you train subs, what do you ask them for?"

For a long minute I studied him, wondering what he was getting at, slightly fearful he'd change his mind and ask me to teach him after all. I wasn't sure I would be able to stay impartial, and that was most definitely what he needed right now. "The very first thing that happens is I sit down with them and talk about what they're looking for."

"And what if they don't know?"

"Then I help them figure it out."

He nodded, thoughtful, then lifted himself up slightly. "I see. May I go up now?"

"Yes. Go on."

I watched him ascend the stairs, heard the bathroom door close, and finally let my breath out. He was too perfect. Snow White with a twist, and unconsciously sexy and eager. No way could I deny I wanted way more of him than was good for him, and I wasn't sure what I was going to do about it.

Hurrying to my office, I picked up my camera on the off chance he'd let me take snapshots of the damage, for evidence, if it came to that. Kane, once he was caught, would be lucky if the cops got him to trial before Rolly did. My own instructions from the club owner were very specific. Find him. Bring him. I didn't ask, and did not want to know what Rolly intended to do with him. Some things I was better off not knowing. It was a function of our relationship Rolly and I were both comfortable with.

I slumped into my chair. That was something to worry about later. Right now, I worried how I was going to deal with my own raging libido and still do what was best for my little prince.

Who isn't yours, Gabe. Get a grip.

Desperate, I picked up the phone, dialled, and waited out the ringing.

"Gabriel Dominick Stark, do you have any idea what fucking time it is?"

"Actually…no."

"Three o'clock in the morning, Gabe. What's going on?"

"I'm in trouble, Jimmy."

A long sigh sounded over the phone, and I heard cloth shuffling.

"What this time?"

"Remember Collin?"

"That little black-haired pixie of yours?"

"Yeah. Him."

"What about him?" The annoyed exasperation was gone from Jimmy's voice. "A dream?"

"I wish. You know about this Kane character. The ass who's terrorising subs—"

"Yeah."

"He left one at Rolly's tonight. He could be Collin's twin."

"Really?"

"Well. No. Just..." I let out a sigh. "This guy, Rory. He's messed up. He's also perfect. And I've known him," I glanced at my watch, "an hour. I'm so lost. Kane did a number on him. I can't, don't dare, touch him. He's fragile. But fuck, Jimmy, he's under my skin already."

"So what the hell do you want from me?"

For a long, silent minute, I wondered if he was actually going to make me say it, then he sighed heavily.

"You so fucking owe me, Gabe. I'll be over in half an hour."

"Thanks, Jimmy. I'll leave the study open."

I knew he would make me pay, too. For the sake of relieving some tension safely, and not at Rory's expense, it would be worth it.

I hung up, climbed the stairs, newly determined not to fall under Rory's unwitting spell.

Mindful of his boundaries and his need for privacy, I knocked softly on the bathroom door and waited for him to open it. When he did, my resolve nearly crumbled. Mark's too-big track pants hung on his hips, held there precariously by the knotted string. Bare toes peeked from the cuffs, and his bare, hairless chest, tight little pink nipples and flat stomach set my heart thumping again. Delicate, delicious colour tinged his cheeks and neck. It didn't hide the fresh bruise blooming under his chin, though,

"I'm a little skinny."

He wrapped one willowy arm around his middle, and I took another, more appraising look. He was right. He was thin, and my lips curled down.

"How long have you been doing Kane's bidding?"

"Umm…three months, I think, since he started chatting with me online." He paused, bit his lip, and shoved ineffectually at the hair flopping in his face. "Four months."

"And how long since you stopped eating properly?" He was cut, or had been, at one point. There was no doubt about that, but the muscles lacked the sharpness of true health.

"I eat."

"Rory, I already told you, you can ask me anything, and I will answer as best I can, but I have to know the truth. You can't lie to me or hold back information. You corrected yourself once already, and that was good. It's important if I'm going to be able to help you. Do you understand?"

I willed him to understand. I desperately wanted him to trust me, and still, the odds of him actually doing so were not in my favour.

"It isn't that easy."

"I know." I set the camera down and sat on the toilet lid, letting him remain standing where he was. "Tonight, you made yourself a delicious sandwich and ate three bites. You love to cook, but you don't eat."

"I can't." He ran one hand over his belly, and his face fell. "Too tense."

"Tell me what happened?"

My old house creaked in the bustling wind, the oak tree outside scratching its branches along the roof. I waited.

"I had a paunch," he said at last. His fingers tensed against his skin. "Not fat, just… Kane hated it. The first time we went out to this fancy restaurant. It was fabulous food. I ate. It was good. He was paying. I had dessert, wine…"

I waited. There was obviously more to the story, but he had to tell it at his own pace.

"After, it was…he didn't say why."

"Why what?"

"Why he strapped me. Hard." He ran his fingers in horizontal flashes across his belly, back and forth, from just below his pecs to dangerously close to his groin, his hand moving faster and faster, and his lips going slack. "I had to figure it out. When he took me to eat, I ate. He strapped. Eventually, I realised. I stopped eating. He'd order all this food. I didn't eat, and…" He shrugged. "There was always something. Always some reason for him to be angry. Something I did or didn't do."

When he raised his face, it was like I could see the hollow cheeks, the sunken eyes that I'd overlooked.

"If I eat more than a few bites…" Again with the shrug. "I didn't want to puke all over your floor. I didn't know if I was supposed to eat. Sorry."

For a long, tense moment, I couldn't find words. I knew the anger would come out in my voice, maybe be taken the wrong way. Finally, I had to focus on my own hands clasped in my lap in order to keep my voice steady and reasonable.

"It's something we'll work on, Rory. If you let me. You've been starving yourself, and you can't continue like this."

"I thought if I got rid of the paunch, it would be better. He'd like me better, stop —" He sighed and sank onto the chair by the tub. "Wrong again." I watched him studying the floor and couldn't look away when his head suddenly popped up. "Did I get anything right? Even one little thing?"

"Please try and understand that you were never in the wrong. He was. In some respects, keeping him even happy enough to not hurt you worse *was* the right thing to do, even though just about everything he asked of you had nothing really to do with you. It was about him, his needs and desires, and he used you like he might any other toy. To further his own pleasure. I'm sorry if that sounds harsh, but truth is truth. He used you. He never cared about you, just what you could give him. That is backwards from everything a good Dom would do. I need you to understand this, if nothing else, Rory, because you are—"

I clamped my mouth shut. I'd let the tirade get away from me, and he was sitting there, wide-eyed and pale, staring at me with slack features. He was in danger of falling into just the same trap with someone else if I couldn't make him see what a beautiful thing he had to offer, and that it was worth waiting for a man who deserved it.

"What? I'm what?"

I couldn't leave him hanging like that. I'd started and I needed to finish. I just didn't know for sure if telling him he was the quintessential sub was a good idea. He was hardwired to serve. I could see it in him, because I'd been trained to look for it, and it screamed out in everything he did and said.

"Everything I've seen in you so far makes me want to protect you, Rory. You want to please so badly, you've put yourself in a bad situation to make someone else happy. It's your Dom's job to look after you, protect you, to give you a safe place to express your desire to serve him." I reached out to run my knuckles down the side of his upturned face. "You deserve someone who understands how lucky he is to be the one you want to serve. Kane has no idea what that's worth."

"You do." He leant forward, eager and bright. "You understand."

How easy it would be to take what he was offering. But he didn't really know what he was offering. Until he understood, I couldn't accept.

"I do understand, Rory. And believe me, it's tempting."

"You don't want me either." He deflated, a pricked balloon, slumped in on himself, and my heart snapped.

"Not true, Rory."

"Forget it." He stood, turned his back, and braced his hands on the shower rod. "Take your pictures. Do whatever. I know Kane never loved me. I know you have to catch him, so just...get it over with."

His voice had lost all its soft uncertainty, turned hard and bitter, and nothing I said elicited a response other than his moving where and how I required in order to take the pictures. Finally, I put the camera down. He remained with his back to me, his arms wrapped low around his middle.

"Rory—"

"Are you done?"

"Yes."

"Good. Do I have to stay here?"

"Not if you don't want to, but I think it's safer for you if you do."

"Where should I sleep?"

I handed him his shirt, which he snapped out of my hand and yanked on over his head.

"This way." I showed him to the spare room next door, indicating the latch hook on the inside of the door with a flick of my finger. This was about him feeling safe, and my own feelings had no place here.

"Thank you." Inclining his head politely, he stood in the middle of the room, arms dangling at his side, head bowed, and waiting for me to leave.

"In the morning, I'll help you with the cream for your back." I watched his reaction carefully.

He didn't look at me.

"After that, I'll take you home."

"Thank you." The dull words thudded into me like fists, leaving bruises.

"Sleep well, Rory."

He just nodded curtly.

I wanted to get through to him that he had the wrong idea, that he wasn't undesirable, but he was tired, oversensitive, and I could only hope in the morning he would be more receptive to what I had to say.

I waited outside his door, but if he even moved, he made no sound. He didn't latch the door. Because he didn't want to lock me out, or he didn't dare, I had no way of knowing. I tried not to take it personally either way.

Back downstairs, I found Jimmy already sitting in my den, playing solitaire on my password-protected laptop. I sighed.

"Jimmy—"

"You need a better password, dude."

"Don't call me dude." I snapped the top of the computer down, and he barely managed to yank his fingers to safety.

"Sugar daddy?" He grinned up at me, showing off a lot of bright, straight teeth. Dark brown eyes danced, and his curly brown hair bobbed around his face. "So, what are we up for today?" He stood, licked his lips suggestively, and unbuckled his belt.

"Very romantic."

"So's calling me up in the middle of the night for a quickie." He shoved his jeans down. The big silver belt buckle hit the carpeted floor with a thump.

I had to hand it to him. He kept me in my place, never letting me ignore my own selfish stupidity. He was one sub who'd never entirely succumb to any Dom. Certainly not to me, though he never said no when I called him.

Now he stood, pants around his ankles, hands clasped at the small of his back, a slight, eager sneer on his face. He liked to be told what to do. In fact, he just liked sex, period, and although he didn't have that same instinct to please as Rory, he did know what I needed, and he offered it enthusiastically enough.

Just looking at him standing there in only his tented boxers made me hard and guilty at the same time.

"Don't." He frowned.

"Don't what?"

"Don't analyse it. I see you over-thinking this." He waggled a finger in my face. "No thinking. Just fucking."

"My brain doesn't turn off for sex."

"It should. At least until after you've ravaged me. I spent the drive over here imagining your hard dick up my ass. You cop out now, you owe me double, and I might not come next time."

"You're just a slave to your own sex drive."

His eyebrows went up. "How is this a bad thing, pot?"

"Never said it was. Turn around and drop 'em."

"Better." He stepped out of his pants, pulled off his boxers, and leaned both hands on my desk. His stance wasn't exactly submissive. It crossed my mind that I was a bit addicted to his tangy tongue and demanding sex drive, that I almost craved the way he egged me on, but we'd learned early on we weren't compatible outside the bedroom, and that was okay.

"You do have a fine ass." I gave it a nice, hard slap, and Jimmy grunted, swayed it from side to side, tipped his hips so it lifted nicely. "Other side?"

"Please."

Some of the defiance had already bled out of his voice, and I spent a little time driving him into a more pliable head space. He was panting hard by the time I had his ass nice and pink and his hole ready. Not that he needed the prep, but it was fun, and a release for me, to watch him squirm his way to the edge of begging.

"Not too loud, now, Jimmy. I have a guest, and I don't want him walking in on anything that might upset him."

"Like you fucking another guy?"

"He's fragile. Shut your mouth and try not to be loud."

Instead of agreeing, he fumbled across the desk into a top drawer and came back with a length of silk scarf that he handed over his shoulder. "Use this."

A slow grin spread over my face. "You please me, Jimmy." I twisted the scarf into a loose rope, and he opened his mouth enough for me to slip it between his lips. "Feeling a little out of control, are we?" Careful not to catch his unruly curls in the knot, I tied the gag behind his head.

Almost instantly, his demeanour changed. His head dropped, his shoulders rounded, and he looked over his shoulder at me as he crossed his arms behind his back. His eyes had taken on a dark, soft expression, somehow needy and generous at once. He didn't often go there, and almost never with me.

I tucked a bit of hair away from his eyes and smiled. "Good God, Jimmy, you can be a beautiful son-of-a-bitch. Now eyes front and spread your legs."

He did, lowering his powerful chest to the desktop and adjusting his ass to the right height so I could take him.

Tremors rippled through him, his inner sub responding to me taking firm hold of his wrists in one hand. I slicked my cock with the other. His breath hissed out as I took him swiftly. Knowing he liked the burn, I still took great care not to really hurt him. His legs shook with the strain of holding himself still. He was giving me all the control — something he never, ever did.

"You're good, Jimmy." I ran my free hand over his back, then started pumping, lavishing touch and praise, practically drunk on having the big man so open to me. I'd trained him. I knew what he liked and what he didn't. I knew he struggled with being powerless, and I had to make sure he knew how much I appreciated it. His voice came in muffled moans from behind the gag, and he turned his head to rest his cheek on the desk. I watched his face, how the sweat on his brow curled the hair there even tighter. After another few, hard strokes, he closed his eyes. His lips moved over the gag, whispered words I couldn't make out, and a sound I'd never before heard from him bubbled up from his chest.

I recognised my name, garbled by the sodden cloth. He muttered it over and over again. His hips started to move, countering me, adding his not inconsiderable power to my own hard thrusts. Then his eyes flew open as every muscle in his body knotted, including his anus, squeezing my dick tight. His cock was pressed hard against the side of the desk, pointed at the floor. I thought the position must have been uncomfortable at the very least, but I felt the warm spatter of cum on my toes, and Jimmy's body began to tremble in earnest. Goose flesh sprang up, and he shivered convulsively.

"Shhh." I gripped his wrists a little tighter, knowing he would want the reassurance of contact and containment, and ran my hand up and down his spine. I could barely breathe through the tight bands of excitement his complete submission caused. It was so rare and all the more precious because he so often kept something back that tonight he was letting go of. "Shh. You're good, Jimmy. Just a little longer. Stay where you are."

He nodded, lifted his hips, and thrust jerkily against me. I reached down to release the gag, and he gasped in a few deep breaths.

"Harder, Gabe. Just…hard. Fuck me, Please."

I obliged, feeling my own peak building rapidly at his plea, and with a few more punishing thrusts, I was coming hard into my condom.

Much as I wanted to fall across him in boneless bliss, one thing he had never been was a cuddler. Instead, I brought my own breathing under control, pulled out, removed the condom and tossed it in the trash can. I braced my weight against his wrists then helped him up.

He was still shaking, standing there with nothing but the soggy gag hanging loosely around his neck.

"Okay?"

He nodded. Sweat glistened over his body, and though I'd shuffled back to give him room to stand, he didn't show any signs of needing more space just yet.

A few quiet minutes passed before he finally turned to face me. He didn't say anything at first, just smoothed the tails of my shirt out of his way and straightened my pants. I let him tidy me up and waited patiently for him to speak.

"So." He kept his eyes on his task, studiously not looking at me, but taking his time about zipping me up.

"So."

He fumbled over the belt, and I reached to place a hand on his cheek.

He looked up. "Beautiful, huh?"

I smiled. "Son-of-a-bitch."

He offered an answering smile, and I couldn't help but kiss it off his face.

"You always know exactly what I need," I said softly.

He just shrugged, slipped out from between me and the desk, and retrieved his own clothes. "This guest of yours—" He pulled on his boxers and ambled over to the wet bar, where he got himself a glass of water and some napkins, which he used to clean his spunk from the floor by my desk. "New project?"

"Not exactly." I went after my own drink, noting how quickly he'd re-established his boundaries simply by not offering me a glass of water. "Kane." I took my drink to my desk and opened the laptop, pulling the camera over and removing the memory card.

"Shit." He slammed the soiled napkins into the trash can. "Bad?"

"Bad enough. I don't think he's ever had any other experiences in the lifestyle. I wasn't kidding about his being fragile. He's a mess."

Jimmy came over and perched on the desk beside me. "You're letting this guy get under your skin, Gabe."

"He's delicate. You didn't see him, Jimmy. He's—"

"I was talking about Kane." This time, he reached for me and turned me to face him with a hand on my jaw. "You tell me who's a little out of control."

I sighed. He could see right through me. He already had, and his performance was his way of trying to balance me out again. "I'm in trouble, Jimmy."

"I can see that."

I pursed my lips, pulled out of his grasp, and brought the pictures I'd taken up on the computer's screen.

Jimmy took the machine and flipped through. "This is fucking brutal."

"I know." It had been all I could do to remain calm when I'd seen Rory's back. Kane hadn't just lashed him. He'd brutalised him. The red welts from tonight were only one layer of the abuse. Yellowed and purple bruises criss-crossed his skin, front and back, and some of the newest marks had broken the skin. I couldn't imagine how the man had walked around straight-backed and acting like he wasn't in excruciating pain.

Jimmy scrolled back through the pictures and stopped on one that showed Rory's face in the mirror. "God damn. He does look like Collin." He shook his head. "Gabe, you gotta let this one go."

"Too late."

It was his turn to let out a sigh. "You cannot save everyone, you hear me?"

"I can save him. He's here. Safe. I can keep him safe."

"You are a delusional freak, Gabriel." He got up from the desk and proceeded to stuff himself back into the rest of his clothing, berating me the entire time. "You're going to latch onto this guy, drive yourself mad trying to mould him into…something. I don't even know what. You can't—" He stopped, glared at me, jacket in hand. "Don't do this, Gabe. Please. Let it go."

"I can't. He needs me."

"He needs help. He doesn't need you trying to replace what you lost with something you can't have."

"You don't understand."

"No." Jimmy crossed the room in three long strides and loomed over me. "I understand perfectly, and you are going to ruin not just him, but—"

I shot up from my chair. "I am not going to hurt him! I'm not stupid. I know he's not Collin. I know. Collin's dead. Gone. This is different. I'm not in love with this guy. I just want to help him!"

Jimmy stood his ground, shaking his head and looking sad, angry, worried. "You're going to get hurt, Gabby. And I won't be able to fix it with a quick fuck or two, no matter how much I give you."

"I don't know if I can do this without you, Jimmy."

"So I should stick around? Watch you dash yourself to pieces over this guy and offer up my ass when the pressure gets too much for you? No thanks." He was already headed for the door and the back yard where he'd left his bike.

"You're right. I won't. No more sex. Just help me out."

He stopped at the doorway but didn't turn around. "How?"

"Buffer."

"Keep you honest, you mean?" He gave me a smouldering look over his shoulder. "Keep you out of his pants? How does that not constitute being the consolation fuck?"

"I already said 'no sex'. Just be here." The idea had only then occurred to me. If I wasn't alone in the house with Rory, I would have a better chance of staying focused on his needs and not my own desires.

"You want me to stay."

The word was anathema to Jimmy. I was asking a hell of a lot more of him to stay platonically than to come over for a midnight fuck, and I knew it.

"You really have lost it already, haven't you?" He turned around and peeled away my shell with just his look.

"I need your help, Jimmy."

"You sure as fuck do." For a long minute, he stood there, looking at me, weighing it all in his mind, then slowly, he put on his jacket. "Go to bed, Gabriel. Get some sleep."

"Jimmy—"

"I'll see you in the morning." He stepped out the French window and was gone.

Chapter Three

Rory

The room wasn't exactly dark, and though Gabe had made a point of indicating the latch hook on the door, I didn't use it. I didn't want to think I had to protect myself from him. I didn't think there was any danger of him sneaking in to ravage me in the middle of the night. He'd as much as rejected me already. He didn't want me any more than Kane did. At least he was honest about it. I gave him that. Kane had done nothing but lie to me from the moment we met.

I flopped onto my back, blinking through the sting and pain, letting it fill me up, and watched the shadows play across the ceiling. A streetlight outside shone through the leafy branches of the poplar tree in Gabe's back yard and tossed ever-changing shadows across the wall and ceiling. Much as I watched those shadows dance, there was never any pattern. The wind moved the leaves in random formations, and from one second to the next, everything changed. Like Gabe. One minute he was tender, and I knew he was going to help me. The next, he was telling me what to do, or telling me no.

He was a Dom. Like Kane. Whatever he said, I had to remember that. One thing he'd said made sense. Kane had never wanted what I wanted. He only looked out for his own needs, and for whatever reason, he had needed me to crawl at his feet, bend myself into a pretzel to figure out what he expected, what he required. Gabe would do the same thing.

And still, I lay there, as though I didn't have the wherewithal to get my own ass to my own house and get on with my life.

"Because you want him, dumbass." I whispered the words into the spiralling shadows, expecting them to echo back at me. The room soaked them up, kept them.

Gabriel Stark was not an easy man to deny. He was everything I thought Kane would be, everything I wanted Kane to be. The only difference was, Kane had taken me. Gabe had turned me down.

"Shit, shit, shit."

I climbed out of the bed and tiptoed to the door. He was probably sound asleep down the hall. I could just walk out. He wouldn't care. I would figure out whatever I had to figure out. I wasn't a complete idiot. Now that I knew what *not* to do, I'd find a Dom, a good one, who wanted me. How hard could it be?

There were no sounds to be heard on the other side of the door. I eased it open and padded down the hall as quietly as possible. By the time I got to the top of the stairs, I heard voices. Muffled voices, but voices just the same. Straining, I tried, but couldn't make out a word. I recognised Gabe's low rumble, but the other vice was not one I knew.

"Obviously. You don't know him, either," I berated myself, listening to the way Gabe's house creaked and whispered, hiding the voices under its own movement.

Part of me wanted to bolt for the front door and never look back. Whoever he was talking to could be anyone. He could be planning anything.

The realisation rocked me. I was just back in the nightmare. Kane's voice echoed in my head, unpleasant and sneering, mixing with the voices of strangers. Those were nights I didn't want to remember. Nights where anyone who wanted to could watch him, watch me, judge how well I obeyed, even punish me for whatever slight they thought they detected. Tests, he'd called them. I always failed. And no one in those places ever thought to ask me if I wanted to be there, on display, doing Kane's bidding.

I crouched at the head of Gabe's stairs, staring down into the bright light below, not really seeing anything at all. What if they had asked? What if someone there had thought to ask the sub if he wanted any of it? What would I have said? I'd have said yes. I wanted to be there. I'd have tried to make Kane see I was being a good boy. Only now did I have a glimmer of understanding that no, I hadn't wanted it. Not like that.

I must have crouched there a good long while. When I shook myself back to reality, the voices had stopped. The house was quiet.

"Gabe?"

Had he left? Maybe I was alone in the house, no one to stop me leaving.

"Gabe?" I got up and moved halfway down the steps, wondering, even as I did, why.

"Rory?" His rumbling voice carried from around the bottom of the stairs, at the back of the house. Then he was there, looking up at me from below, a worried look on his face. "I thought you were asleep."

I shook my head. "Can't. You?"

He shook his head, too.

I sat down, aware I was trembling. "I'm tired." I hadn't really meant to say it out loud. The habit of talking to myself was one I'd never really kicked, or moderated. I was alone enough of the time anyway.

"Then go back to bed. It's the middle of the night."

"I just lie there, watching the shadows on the walls."

Gabe nodded, his eyes never leaving my face. I wondered what he was looking for. "I'm not keeping you here, Rory. If you want to go, I'll call you a cab."

"Just an hour ago, you wanted me to stay. For my own safety."

"And I still do, but I thought we established this isn't about what I want. It's about what you need, and if you need to go home, then I'll arrange that."

"I'll just go back to the shadows." I didn't want to admit it to him, but whether he wanted me or not, I still felt safer here, with him, than I did even thinking about my own house. At least here, I wasn't alone and Kane had no idea where I was. I got up and returned to my room.

"Rory."

His voice, coming from the other side of my closed door, blended and meshed with the shadows, taking the spooky emptiness away and replacing it with a bit of living, breathing calm.

"What?"

Silence.

Maybe if I lay there and didn't say anything, he'd go away and I wouldn't have to hear him say, yet again, he didn't want me.

The silence stretched.

I thought he had to have gone away when he finally spoke.

"I want to help you. I want to make this right. I can only do that if you want it, too. I'll only try if you allow it. So if you're here for breakfast in the morning, I will assume that you are willing to try. If that's the case, we will sit down and talk, and you will tell me everything I need to know. You'll answer all my questions with the truth, and we can go from there."

I strained, listening in the dark for some sign he remained outside my door or had gone back to whatever it was he did in the middle of the night when he couldn't sleep. A long time passed before light peeked around the blinds at my window and thin grey fingers of morning crawled across the floor.

When it was light enough to see without turning on any lights, I tiptoed out of the room. The small bathroom we had used the night before stood empty, but the other door along the hallway at the top of the stairs was closed. I took a few minutes to wash the dried, lonely night off me and went down to the kitchen.

An hour later, when Gabe plodded down the stairs and deposited himself in the same kitchen chair he'd sat in last night, I had most of a pancake breakfast cooked and waiting. I set a glass of orange juice and a mug of coffee down in front of him.

"You drank it black last night, so..."

He nodded. "Thanks. This is good."

Tension rose with the vapour of his drink, wafted over the air on heat and steam as I opened the oven to bring out the warm cakes. I set the platter down amongst the condiments already arranged on the table and went back for the bacon.

Once I was seated across from him, he finally spoke. "I'm glad you stayed."

"Really?" I jammed my fork into a pancake and tossed it onto his plate. "Because you could have fooled me. What with the thanks but no thanks last night, and the silent treatment—"

"Enough." He didn't raise his voice or move a muscle.

My hand froze, midair, in the act of spearing another pancake, and I dropped my gaze to trace the weave of the placemat under my plate. Slowly, I pulled my arm back, set the fork down, and folded my hands in my lap. I couldn't say why I was so freaked out. He hadn't yelled. Hadn't raised a finger to reprimand me physically. He just sat there, watching me, and the longer I waited, the worse it got.

"Let's start here, Rory. You respect my space, and I respect yours. Right now, my reasons for saying no last night are my own. I'm not obligated to explain."

"No, Sir." He wasn't. It was my own pathetic need to know why he didn't want me, what was wrong with me that even he couldn't be bothered, that had prompted my attack. "I'm sorry."

He leant forward, the motion catching my attention and drawing my head up. When I met his gaze, it wasn't hard, cold, like I expected. I couldn't really tell what he was feeling, but there was no anger.

"Believe it or not, I understand why you're pissed off. I also understand why you offered yourself last night, and it would have been the height of disrespect for me accept."

"But I wanted—"

"When you truly understand what it was you offered me last night, there's every chance I will accept it, Rory. Right now, you have no idea—"

"You think I'm an idiot, don't you?" If he was trying to appease me somehow, he wasn't going to have much luck telling me I had no idea what I even wanted, or who I wanted in my own bed. I was a grown man. So I'd made a mistake with Kane. I'd learned my lesson.

"Do you think you're an idiot?"

His question caught me completely off-guard, and I fumbled. "Well...I..." Unthinking, I slumped back in my chair, gasping at the unexpected zing of pain, and straightened again. "I made a stupid mistake."

"That isn't what I asked."

Last night, he'd stipulated that the only requirement on my part was that I tell him the truth when he asked me a question. He wanted me to sit there and confess I thought I was a complete fool for falling for Kane and letting him do what he did.

When I didn't answer, he settled back, coffee in hand, and sighed. "You aren't alone in not wanting to admit you feel like a fool. I've been trying to catch Kane for months, and I don't even know what the guy looks like."

"So you want me here to help you find him."

A look passed over his face. I couldn't begin to decipher it, but he didn't say anything.

"If I tell you everything I can remember, I should get something in return." I didn't know what I was doing. I just knew I wanted to show him I could be good, worthy, that if he gave me a chance, he might actually like me.

"Something like what?" He sounded wary, and the coffee mug came up to cover his face so I couldn't read his expression.

"You show me how it's supposed to go."

His eyes narrowed, and his nostrils flared. "How what is supposed to go?"

"Teach me how to be a good sub."

Gabe leant forward, set his mug down and pressed up, palms flat against the table so he could loom, right in my face. "Learn how to face your mistakes and insecurities. Learn how to take no for an answer, and be strong enough to tell the truth. Do you think you're an idiot?"

"No!" I pushed back, knocking my chair over in my haste to stand and remove myself from his shadow. "I made a rookie mistake. A naïve, stupid, dangerous misjudgement of Kane's character." I squared my shoulders and met his eye. "I'm not doing that here. Give me a chance. Please."

"What makes you think you can trust me? Why do you think I'm any different?"

I didn't have any proof he was anything at all. Just gut instinct, and when I compared that to my initial reaction to Kane, it told me Gabe was a completely different kind of person. I shrugged. "I don't know…"

"No. You don't. You can't, because you haven't known me long enough. Besides…" He came around the table, and although I backed up, he kept coming until my shoulder bumped against the fridge and I had nowhere else to go.

I didn't want to be afraid of him. Yet I couldn't stop my heart pounding or the cold sweat breaking out between my shoulders. I couldn't look away from the penetrating, steely grey of his eyes.

"You seem to think I can make you into something, that you're lacking something I can teach you. I don't teach people how to be subs. I let them be who they are and I teach them how to find the right kind of Dom."

"I don't understand."

He nodded. The smell of soap mixed with the morning's residue of sleepless nights surrounded me as he leaned a little bit closer. I breathed it in, closed my eyes, searched for the clean, pure scent that would be Gabe under the stale leftovers of last night.

He was not trying to frighten me. That was my own reaction, and I forced myself to control it. I pulled in a deep breath, and some of the warmth and that soapy, edgy scent infused my senses again. It was a good smell, safe, without the stink of aggression and anger Kane always carried with him in his sweat.

"I know you don't. But in time, you will." A light touch, fingers riding smoothly along my jaw, prompted me to turn my head, seeking more.

I parted my lips, feeling the warmth of Gabe's breath mingle with my own. I'd never wanted a kiss more in my life. The need for it throbbed through me. I felt a moan build in my chest, but it lodged behind my breath, coming in short little pants.

Gabe's thumb made a featherlight pass over my bottom lip.

A crisp knock on the kitchen door made us both jump. Gabe landed about three feet away, and I wilted against the cool stainless steel of the refrigerator. A few thudding heartbeats passed before he moved to answer the knock.

"Rory, will you please make more pancakes? We have a guest."

I nodded, willed my legs to take my weight, picked up my fallen chair, and went about the task assigned. It was good to have a concrete direction to take as Gabe let his guest in. Slowly, I managed to bring the shaking of my hands under control as I gathered ingredients and concentrated on something I did know, and was confident I was good at.

The man who sauntered into our kitchen—Gabe's kitchen—was tall. *Handsome*, I supposed, but not in the same dark, electric-eyed way Gabe was. He had a surfer look, with baggy shorts and a worn T-shirt, shaggy hair that fell over brown eyes, and a slouch Kane would have beaten out of me without mercy.

"Jimmy Phillips," Gabe gestured to me, "this is Rory Sanders. Rory, my friend, Jimmy."

"Hey." Jimmy held out a big, square hand.

Mine, thankfully, was covered in flour. No need to actually touch him, and no risk of looking as nervous as I felt, or appearing to snub him. I nodded, and he smiled.

"Get yourself a wife there, Gabe?"

My jaw dropped, but Gabe gave him a quelling glare before I managed to protest myself.

"Jimmy, be nice."

"Sure. Whatever." The big man gave a shrug and turned to Gabe. "I need to...um...hang out. For a bit." His gaze dropped to the floor, and though he hung his head slightly, it didn't give the impression of shame or uncertainty. It just looked like his version of appearing humble. As if a person could be humble when he towered over everyone in the room and brought with him an air of strength and power like this guy did.

Gabe frowned, glanced at me, and I quickly dropped my gaze back to my task. It wasn't my place to utter a word, but my heart sank. Another body in this small house about dashed any hope I might have had of winning Gabe over. The disappointment speared me, turning my gut inside out.

"How long is a bit?" Gabe asked.

Jimmy shrugged. "Few days. I don't know."

"Rory?" Gabe sidled up, putting himself between me and Jimmy, and I was ashamed to feel the relief melt through me and some of my tension ease. "Do you mind if Jimmy sleeps on the couch a few nights?"

"Not my couch," I mumbled.

"Listen, dude, if I make you uncomfortable—"

"You don't!" I whirled, stepping past Gabe and glaring up at him. "This is not my house. Makes no difference to me who Gabe takes in." I drew in a deep breath, aware the outburst proved it did matter. But determined not to back down, not to show my disappointment at the intrusion, I looked Gabe in the eye and attempted a smile. "He's your friend, right? And he needs your help. You should help him."

"I want you to feel comfortable about this."

"Does it really matter how I feel? I do have my own house. I can go home any time I want, right?"

"Of course."

"Then it isn't an issue. Please. Sit down and drink your coffee before it gets cold. Jimmy? Would you like a cup?" I reached for a mug in the cupboard, but he shook his head.

"That shit rots your insides, dude. You got milk?"

"Of course."

I was pretty sure if he called me 'dude' one more time, I might pour the milk over his lovely, wavy hair, but in actual fact, it was good to feel that kind of honest, clean annoyance at something admittedly silly. For once in a very long time, I felt like myself—the person I had forgotten how to be when Kane came along. It was a relief to know I was still in there inside my own skin somewhere.

Gabe

Jimmy could not have arrived at a more opportune moment. It wouldn't be so hard to resist my own want for Rory if he didn't throw himself at me every time I turned around. I could feel Jimmy's appraisal and knew the minute he got me alone he'd be counselling me to get Rory out of the house, get my distance from him. And he'd be right. It was the best advice, the advice I'd give anyone in my situation.

Sure as shit, after breakfast, Jimmy cornered me in the den, and the minute we were alone, his gaze turned sharp and he loomed. He liked to use his height like that.

"What?"

He snorted.

"Well…" I snarled. Defensive, I knew, but I was on the defence. "Now you understand."

"I understand you're up to your eyeballs in it, Gabby."

I sighed and sank into my chair. "So what do I do? Send him home? Let him work all this shit out on his own? You know how hard it is to find the right balance."

"And I was never that…"

This time, I snorted. "You were never *that*," I agreed.

"Gabe, some people can figure this out on their own. Some, no matter how smart they are, just can't be trusted to keep their own best interests at heart."

"He is smart. And strong." I clamped my jaw tight, thinking of what Rory had endured already. "And completely incapable of saying no."

"Kane doesn't accept no. He doesn't teach it, doesn't allow it. Rory probably doesn't realise he can, and sometimes *should*, refuse a Dom's advances."

I shook my head. Jimmy was as adept at reading other Doms as I was, maybe more so, because he'd been with so many and knew there were as many different ways to submit as there were people to submit to.

"And he won't say no to you, either, Gabe, so you have to say it for him."

"I know. I have. He keeps trying, and Lord help me, Jimmy, I don't know how many times I *can* say no."

"As many as it takes until he stops asking."

"And then what?" I looked up, caught his eye. The sympathy on his face told me he could tell I knew that if I got it through to Rory I wasn't his Dom, couldn't be, I'd also get it through to him that I didn't want him. Nothing could have been further from the truth.

"Ask yourself this — do you want to fuck him, or do you want to help him?"

"Jesus."

"Well. Let your little head do the thinking for you, Gabby, and sure as shit you'll do him more harm than Kane ever did, because he trusts you. He wants you, and he knows you have the potential to be what he thought he was looking for in Kane. You said it yourself. He's not stupid. He's vulnerable. You're the Dom here. Act like it."

"You just love being right, don't you?"

To my surprise, Jimmy shook his head. "Not when it hurts you this much, no. But right now, you can take it. He can't, so suck it up."

For a long time, we both sat there, quiet, while I stared off into space and poked at the ache of wanting what I couldn't have.

"I need you to do something for me," I said at last.

I expected him to give me grief, because that was Jimmy's MO. He just nodded.

"Take him home."

Jimmy's brows shot up. "Really? He looked to me like he was settling in."

"He should go home. If he wants to come back, bring him back, but if he walks around in those joggers falling off his hips much longer... For fuck's sake, I'm only human. He needs his own clothes, and we need access to his laptop and all the websites and chat rooms he's been to." I fixed Jimmy with an appraising look. "You can handle that? I can call Gina, if you like."

"Let's just play it by ear. If he looks like he's gonna stay there, I'll call Gina myself. He knows her?"

"Yeah. He's okay with her."

"Then maybe if he decides not to come back here, she can talk him into calling someone to stay with him awhile."

I nodded. I had no idea if Kane would seek him out, but Rory had said the bastard knew his address. Kane's typical MO was to never contact them again after he did this disappearing act. It was the ultimate rejection that broke most of his conquests, but I had an unpleasant feeling Rory was different. For one, the abuse reflected in the bruises over his body spoke of a much longer association than Kane had had with most of his other victims. For another, after studying the lash marks, I was convinced that Rory was more to him than just another fuck. The way he'd plied the whip was not just a punishment. It was something else, something that had more meaning to Kane if the pattern of criss-crossed welts was any indication. It wasn't — quite — random enough to be a simple lashing. Something in my gut told me he could not be allowed to get his hands on Rory again.

"What are you thinking?" Jimmy leant forward and rested his arms on the desk in front of me.

"Don't leave him there alone. If he won't call anyone, make sure Gina stays with him. Or bring him back here."

"You think Kane will come looking for him?"

"I don't know. I don't want to take the chance that he does and Rory's alone."

"You think Rory would actually even let him in the door after last night?"

I eyed him. "What do you know about last night?"

Both Jimmy's hands came up in defence. "I work for Rolly, too, Gabe. He briefed us all, and Gina knew I was here last night. She told me the details." He tossed himself negligently back in the chair. "For some reason, she thought you might call me to babysit, and she didn't want me going into this," he wagged a finger between us, "blind."

Annoyance tugged my lips down and sent a worm of tension up through my neck. My sister was a royal pain in the ass sometimes. "She had no business breaching Rory's privacy."

"Call it looking out for a friend, then. We all know you have a tendency to leave that part out of your equation sometimes."

"Hey. You don't *have* to come when I call."

He stood, shaking his head, and reached for his straw cowboy hat that went absurdly well with the baggy shorts and top. "Actually, Gabe, I do."

Before I could even ask what the hell that meant, he was flopping out of the room, his sandals slapping against the bare bottoms of his feet. It's not like I ever held a gun to his head, or even said word one when he refused me. If he figured he had to answer the phone, or say yes when I asked for him, that was on him.

I listened to his bass voice explain things to Rory. I wasn't up to facing either of them for the time being, but Rory came into the den about ten minutes later, arms crossed over his chest, long black hair dangling in his eyes.

"Why aren't you taking me?"

I bit down on the inside of my cheek. I had never asked him for obedience. He had every right to come and go as he pleased and make whatever challenges he wanted.

"I have work to do."

"I can wait."

"Jimmy's free now."

"If you send me home with him, I'm not coming back."

"That's your choice." I looked up, finally, though the computer screen I had been staring at only showed the blank load-up screen. "You're not a prisoner. You do whatever makes you feel most comfortable. But…"

"But?" he prompted, after I stopped looking for a way to present my argument that didn't sound like I was trying to influence him either way.

"If you don't come back here, please, please find someone who can stay with you for a few days, at least."

"So you are worried about me?"

"Of course, Rory. I'd be worried about anyone in your situation. I just want you to be safe."

His lips tightened, and the muscles of his arms hardened as he increased his grip on himself. "You can't deny it's more than that," he insisted.

I waited. I could see the more he wanted me to admit to in his dark eyes, I could see what he wanted, and I knew I wanted to answer it. But I waited. He had to learn how to ask, then had to learn to accept the answer he got.

"This morning. You were going to kiss me."

I nodded.

"I wanted you to."

"I know."

"So why didn't you?"

"Because." I closed the computer and got up, knowing I was taking a chance, not keeping the safe bulk of the desk between us. "You don't need me, or anyone else, kissing you right now."

His eyes went wide. "You don't know what I need."

I settled my ass against the desk and crossed my own arms even as his fell away. "Actually, I do. This is what I do, Rory, and if you can't accept that I know what's best right now, then perhaps it is better if you don't come back."

"You can't." He took a few shuffling steps closer. "I didn't mean that. Please don't throw me out."

"Go with Jimmy now. Think about it. If you come back, I will assume you trust me enough to teach you how to handle yourself around a proper Dom, and how to recognise people like Kane before you're in trouble."

He nodded.

"If you come back, bring some clothes and your computer, but nothing else. And understand this." I paused, waiting for him to meet my gaze and acknowledge my authority. "I will make the decisions as to how, when and *if* anything physical happens. Is that understood?"

He nodded faintly, his eyes still wide, dark pools.

I wanted to reassure him I was doing it because I cared very much that he heal whole, on the off chance he still wanted me as much then as he thought he did now, but I couldn't add that pressure, that enticement, to his precarious balance right now.

"Go with Jimmy."

He nodded again but didn't move.

Drawing in a deep breath of the morning air, warmed by the sun slicing through the room from the windows, I approached him and risked laying a hand on his shoulder. Encouraged by the fact that he didn't look away, I cupped his chin, just needing to touch him, to reassure myself that he was real, solid, and not my wet-dream hallucination. "Promise me you'll think about what I said."

"I will, Gabe." He tipped his head delicately, resting his cheek against my palm for just an instant before he stepped back. "I'll think about it. And I'll make lunch when I get back."

There was no disguising the fact my smile reflected my relief. I wanted him back, and he knew it. I could see the glimmer of knowledge in his eye. He knew the kind of power he wielded. Knowing I wanted him, even though I couldn't admit it out loud, even though I couldn't assure him it was true, it still gave him a great deal of satisfaction, and he smiled back before turning to walk calmly out of the room.

"Tell Jimmy to take my car!" I called after him. My overly protective instincts didn't want to take any chances with either of them on Jimmy's bike with Jimmy's pissy mood and lack of reasonable care when he was distracted.

Jimmy

While Rory went in to 'chat' with Gabe, I dug out my cell and dialled Gina.

"You were right," I shot at her as soon as I heard the click of her picking up. I cringed at how ungrateful I sounded. Downright petulant.

"Oh, man, Jim, it's fucking early."

"Suck it up." I sprawled into an uncomfortable Adirondack on Gabe's porch and squirmed until I was less uncomfortable. "The tension is unbearable. They'll be fucking any minute."

"You can't let that happen, Jimmy. Not yet."

"I hate to inform you, dearie, but I can't stop it. This is a fucking force of nature, and I'm just going to get swept out to sea. I'm nobody here."

"I'm sorry, baby. Come home. Let Gabby sink his own ship."

I let out a sigh, switched ears, and dropped my forehead into my hand. "You know I can't do that, Gee. Gabe's too good to just take, and holding back is killing him." I paused, but she said nothing. "I have never felt more inconsequential in my life." *It completely sucks.*

"Don't let him take advantage of you, Jimmy. He's no saint, and you are not a consolation prize."

"I should say no to Gabe the God?" I wasn't going to get all emotional on her, but she knew better than that. "You know I can't do that."

"I know you deserve better."

Maybe I called her because she got it. She cared what I was going through, but didn't judge me for putting myself through it anyway.

"I'll be here, Jimmy," she said after I made no response. "For God's sake, honey, please do not get yourself in the middle. If it's real between them—"

I snorted. "I'm not watching them, if that's what you're getting at. If it's real, I'll be out the door faster than you can say *sayonara*. But if it falls apart, Gabe will need a friend."

"Do you think it will?"

"Honestly?" I drew up my mental picture of the black-haired sprite, tried to draw devil's horns on the image, and grimaced. "I don't know. Hard to say how much damage Kane did, really, until we get to know Rory, but I don't think he's as fragile as Gabe thinks he is. That will either glue them together or fuck up the whole thing when he finds his backbone again. But he's halfway to domesticated already, and I highly doubt Gabe had anything to do with that."

"So…"

"So…either he's fucking perfect and I'm screwed, or it's good it was Gabe's idea I come back, because if Kane has done this, and Rory is his creature, Gabe is never going to see it."

Again, she remained quiet.

"I'd rather be the one left out in the cold, Gee. If Gabe gets hurt like that again…" Even Doms could be broken.

"I don't want that for you, Jimmy."

I smiled at her concern. I swear if she were a guy, my problems would be solved. Drawing in a breath I hoped was not shaky enough to interpret over the phone, I tried to make the best of it. "We both know I'd only ever get scraps from Gabe anyway. I mean, maybe it's time, right? Maybe it's just time to help him find his forever guy and move on."

"And what about your forever guy?"

"It isn't Gabe. Never was. I've been fooling myself long enough."

"You know our couch is always open to you, honey."

"Thanks, Gee."

I suppose that was another point I should look at. My life was a series of one-night stands and friend's couches. Time I put on my big boy pants and figured my own shit out.

I don't know if Rory overheard anything of my conversation, but he was there when I hung up, clomping through the door and handing me Gabe's car keys.

"I have my bike."

"Gabe said no bike."

"Mother fucking hen. You ready, dude?"

"Don't call me dude." He stomped down the steps and waited for me to unlock the car.

Great. This was going to be oodles of fun. I could already tell.

Chapter Four

Rory

Jimmy was a good enough guy. I guess he knew his size was intimidating because he seemed to be going out of his way to be non-threatening. Still, every time he glanced at me from the corner of his eye, I could see he was sizing me up, wondering.

"You keep looking at me like that," I said at last.

"Like what?"

"Like the competition."

I expected him to make some sort of derisive comment. He didn't. He just watched the traffic and remained silent.

"You don't have to worry. He made it pretty clear there's nothing but purely professional interest going on. He wants to find Kane, and I want to help him."

"You're not a very good liar."

"This is me." I pointed to the long, low brick bungalow on the right, and Jimmy pulled into the drive. "Fine. But the interest is all one sided. He said he'd help me. Teach me what I need to know. Because," I made air quotes, "that's what he does."

I wasn't sure I was telling the complete truth, but the fact remained, however he felt, Gabe hadn't admitted to it, so it didn't matter. He wouldn't act on it, either, so it might as well not exist. It was easier to think he just wanted to stop Kane than that he didn't want me.

Jimmy turned off the car and turned in his seat to glare at me. So much for non-threatening. "It *is* what he does, and he's very, very good at it. He can help you if you listen to him and stop trying to get under his skin and into his pants."

"Right. Because that's exclusively your territory."

The scowl Jimmy directed at me set the hairs on the back of my neck standing on end. He shook his head. "Gabe and I. It isn't like that."

"One thing everyone seems to think. That I'm completely clueless. I'm a grown man, and I certainly wasn't a virgin when I met Kane. At least, not in the traditional sense. I know when two guys have a thing."

"A thing? Fuck." Yanking the keys out of the ignition, Jimmy got out and slammed the door.

I was right behind him. "Yeah. A thing. I'd say relationship, but I'm pretty sure that term might be overstating the fact a trifle." I followed him up the walk, almost jogging to match his long stride. A little voice in my head told me I was being unreasonable. I quashed it.

The geraniums by the door dipped sadly, almost kissing the lips of their pots. I felt a pang for having neglected them.

I was still looking at them, and trying to banish the thought of Jimmy and Gabe together, when Jimmy's hand hit me square in the chest and stopped me cold.

"You always leave the inside door open?" he asked.

"No. Never."

"Back in the car." Jimmy turned me around and marched me back the way we'd come.

My heart thudded, and only in part because of the idea someone else had been inside my home. Most of the palpitations stemmed from Jimmy's vice grip on my upper arm and the fact that, even had I the will to try, I would never have freed myself from his grasp. After last night, especially after last night in the club, the idea of not being able to free myself made me break out in a cold sweat and gooseflesh. I squirmed in Jimmy's hold, but he didn't let go. The car beeped, and he had the door open and me inside before I could haul in enough breath to keep from hyperventilating.

He jogged around to the other side and got in himself. The door locks clicked in place. "Think, Rory. Are you absolutely sure you locked both doors?"

"Positive." I wagged my hand in the air, still trying to catch my breath. "It's a thing. I'm sure." My voice fell and got muffled between my feet.

"A thing?" Jimmy's big hand rested between my shoulder blades. "You okay?"

"No. Don't touch me."

He withdrew his hand.

After another minute, I sat up and felt the heat rise into my cheeks, but I nodded. "Paranoia, maybe. The doors are only ever unlocked when I'm physically going through them. And I didn't...mean to snap. My back is...tender."

"It's okay. Sorry about manhandling you. Stupid of me."

I shrugged, wanting to say it was no big deal, but the words wouldn't come. My heart wouldn't stop pounding, and though I knew there was no threat, I couldn't stop the urge to press my shoulder against the door and put as much space between us as possible.

Jimmy took out his cell and dialled three numbers. I sat in numb silence while he reported the break-in. After that, he dialled another number and told someone else.

"Who?"

"A friend. Don't worry. He's a cop, too, and he needs to know about this. He lives in the Alley."

"Oh." A gay cop, then. Not common, and almost never out. Maybe it was good to have him on alert.

We waited, quiet for a long while after he hung up the phone.

"There's no question," he said at last. "You're going back to Gabe's. You can't stay here."

"I want to see."

"Stay put. We don't know when this happened. There could be someone still in there, for all we know. I'm not going in to find out. That's what cops do."

"It's my house!" But his mention of someone still being inside gave me pause and I didn't try to unlock the car door. "Do you think it was Kane?"

"Do you?"

"I wouldn't have thought…" Tipping my head back against the car seat, I closed my eyes and concentrated a moment more on breathing."Then again, before last night, I thought I was the only one…"

"So put it this way. Could it have been anyone else?"

I shook my head. "Who? I draw manga. Most of my work I do at home and send in the mail to my publisher. I do everything else online. I don't know anybody." No point in hiding my friendless state at this point. Cops asked a lot of questions, and one way or another, it would come out I was a complete recluse since I'd met Kane, and the few friends I had made after moving here had written me off as a lunatic and a pervert for wanting to submit to him. The lunatic part I got, now. The pervert part… I glanced at Jimmy. No one I'd met at the club had judged me on being submissive, just on being a fool. Jimmy had issues with me wanting Gabe, but I suspected that was more a jealousy thing than a judgement of my character.

"You gave Kane your address," he said after another tense silence.

"I did. I'd been talking to a lot of people, but he lives in the same city as me, and I was desperate to make a complete fool of myself. The vast majority of the people I speak to online live in a different country. Unless it's just shitty luck to be broken into on the same night as I get my ass chained to a nightclub sex rack, who else could it have been?" I could feel him looking at me and I rolled my head around to look back. "What?"

"If you could just pick."

"Pick what?"

He shook his head, chuckled, and let out a deep sigh. Instead of keeping at me with that intense, demanding glare, he settled his own head against the back rest of his seat and fixed his attention on a small bird flitting in and out of my hedge. "One minute you're this panicked, cowed little submissive, and the next, you're spitting fire and defiance. It would be nice to know which way you're going to land so I could hate you properly."

"First of all, I'm not cowed. You freaked me out, and someone, probably a man who is going to be furious he didn't find me, broke into my house. A mild panic attack was in order. And second," I let out a sigh of my own, "if I have to give up speaking my mind to be submissive, then maybe it isn't what I want after all."

"Any Dom worth anything will not only insist you speak up, but expect it and cherish it."

"Kane didn't."

"I think we've established Kane is a psychopath, and you're lucky he made the mistake of leaving you at Rolly's. There are far less reputable fetish clubs he could have taken you to." He twitched. A spasm of tension shot through him and his big body convulsed a tiny bit.

I watched his chest heave a few times, and almost wanted to reach over and touch his hand, curled into a tight fist on his thigh.

"You don't want to be left alone and helpless in places like that." The moment passed, and he turned to look at me. "The cops are going to want to ask a lot of questions," he said, as though nothing had happened.

I nodded and turned to gaze back out the window. Obviously, Gabe needed a sign above his office door — "Shelter for abused subs". But Jimmy wanted his privacy, so I let him have it. I understood how that went.

"The very first of which will be, where were you all night," he continued.

"I know."

"You can't lie to them."

"No shit." Outside, mid-morning cast a bright, fresh glow over the street and neighbours' lawns. It wasn't the soft glow of dawn anymore, but not yet as warm as the day was going to be either. "At some point, I'm going to have to tell them this. I'll just have to put on my big boy pants and do it."

"We're all on your side, Rory."

"You hate me, remember?"

He sighed and turned his head to look out his window where I couldn't see his face. "I wish."

"For what it's worth. I'm sorry. I didn't know —"

"Nothing to know." He drew himself out of his slump and turned back, a big, fake smile on his face. "Old news, dude. History that should never be repeated."

85

"Still—"

"He's your problem now. Fixated on you, for whatever reason, and that's not necessarily a bad thing. Just don't fuck with him, or Kane will seem like your sugar daddy when I'm through."

I studied his face. There was no hint there of anything but false goodwill. I had no idea what was under it, or if that was a real threat. Not that I had any intention of hurting Gabe. I already thought I might be in love with him. But Jimmy was obviously in love with him, too, and that was going to be a problem.

"I won't," I assured him, hoping if anything *did* go wrong, he understood it wasn't because I wanted it to.

He just nodded. "That aside, we all want Kane caught. Truce?"

"Truce." Better than hostility. "I've lived in the world my whole life, Jimmy. I know how to keep my head down and I won't say anything about Gabe other than he was kind enough to make sure I was okay and give me a safe place to crash."

"They'll ask what else he did. At some point. Not today, but eventually."

"I know. And I'll tell the truth. He took me home, gave me a safe place to get my head together."

"Some cops don't think the fetish community is safe at all. They think it should be illegal, and they treat it that way. They treat Gabe that way."

"And some people don't think ass-fucking should be legal, either. I've lived on the outside my entire life. I'm not going to put Gabe in any homophobic cop's path, believe me."

"Sorry."

"Don't worry about it." I understood his worry. I did. But I didn't need his tension fuelling my own.

Thankfully, a cop car rounded the bend as silence once again thickened the air in the car, and I got out, trying hard not to show my relief.

Jimmy got on the phone again as I stepped onto the drive, no doubt calling Gabe to let him know what was going on. I greeted the cops, who told me to get back in the car while they investigated. I did.

"Gabe's on his way."

"He didn't have to drop everything to come."

Jimmy tilted his head. "Really."

I shrugged. "You're here."

He actually grinned at me. "Yeah. Dude, *I* want Gabby here for this. Trust me. You want him to deal with this for you. Not all cops like him, but he's good at his job, and he works with them all the time. Plus, if it was Kane, he needs to be here. There's a possibility he will find something that will help track this asshole down."

Eventually, the cops came to give us the all-clear, and I was allowed to go inside. Jimmy waited on the porch for Gabe to show up.

Everything inside was destroyed. Everything I owned had been smashed, torn, shattered and ruined. People had called my home austere. Plain. Boring. I liked it that way. Uncluttered. Now, it was mayhem. In pieces, my meagre belongings looked like a whole lot more than they were. My life, spread out in a shambles before me, suddenly resembling on the outside what it had turned into on the inside. I didn't even know where to start.

"We'll need to know if anything is missing," a cop told me.

I nodded. Figuring that out would take days. Weeks, maybe.

"And if you could go and look in the bedroom, there something there you need to see. Tell us if it means anything to you."

"Sure."

I was just picking my way through my destroyed bedroom at the detective's behest when Gabe appeared on the threshold.

"Hey," he said softly, gingerly finding an empty space to step and making his way across the floor.

I was standing by the bed. The mattress, with its white, Egyptian cotton fitted sheet was the only thing in the room not smashed or torn to pieces and strewn on the floor. Attached to each bed post was a cuff, held in place by heavy chain. On the pillow sat an antique wooden ball gag, complete with teeth marks bitten deep into the grain. The leather was oiled and appeared supple, the buckle shimmering in the sunlight. If a person had been spread out in those cuffs, where his groin would rest was the whip Kane had used on me the night before. And to top it all off was a used condom, tied into a neat knot and lying about where a person's chest would be.

"The cops wanted me to look, before they moved anything. To see if it meant anything to me."

Gabe's hand rested on my back, just between my shoulder blades. No doubt he felt the sweat soaking through my shirt and the uncontrolled tremors. "Does it?"

I shook my head. It didn't mean anything more to me than it would to anyone seeing it. It wasn't specific to anything Kane and I had done together, other than that being the same whip. "It's some sort of warning, though, isn't it?"

"I'm inclined to think so." He snuck his arm around my shoulders. "I have to insist you not stay here."

Not like I was going to now. I nodded and leaned against him, grateful for the support when he didn't push me away. Before, I'd been angry, feeling foolish and stupid. Now I was scared. It was the same jolting, mind-numbing feeling I'd had so many times, staring at the floor, my hands shackled and Kane's heavy boots plodding in a slow circle around me. Not knowing when—*if*—the whip was going to fall, or where it would strike, reduced me to quivering uncertainty. Never knowing what small thing he was going to find to punish me for, or if he was going to call some other stranger in to witness my humiliation—or even add to it—had hollowed me out. Every time he fastened the cuffs, I sank into that empty, soulless place. My own home felt like an extension of it now.

"I have to—"

I bolted. Ploughing through the debris of my life, I stumbled for the door and the fresh air and sunlight. Jimmy jumped out of the way as I passed. I didn't stop until I was standing, still shaking, on the front lawn. Gabe was there in an instant, his hands on my shoulders, his intense grey eyes searching my face.

"Talk to me?"

For a long time, I just stood there, eyes glued to his lips, watching them move, knowing he was talking to me, but unable to hear anything beyond the high buzz in my head. How many times had I wanted to do what I'd just done, and run from the agony of that blank space? I'd never been able to escape it before. Never had the freedom to walk away. I'd never even recognised the feeling for the soul-searing fear that it was.

"He was in my house," I muttered, knowing the words tumbled from my mouth even though I couldn't quite hear them. "If I'd been here…"

"You weren't." Gabe gave me a little shake. "Rory, you weren't here. You were safe."

"With you."

He nodded.

"I have to go back in." Finally, I managed to raise my gaze past his lips to his eyes. "They want to know if anything is missing. Will you?"

"Of course."

It turned out the only thing obviously missing was my computer. My flat screen TV, newly purchased with money I'd saved for over a year, my electronics, all my art supplies, everything I could think of that had value, and everything else besides, was smashed to junk.

Any information we might have gleaned from my computer that would have helped Gabe find Kane was gone with it.

"Don't worry about it. We'll log on tomorrow and you can retrace your steps, figure out where you went and who you talked to. It'll take a little longer, but we'll do it together."

"It wasn't our only chance, right?" I was sitting in Gabe's front seat, headed back to his house while the police finished their investigation. Jimmy followed on his bike. "We'll find him?" I wanted reassurance Gabe couldn't really give me, but I felt more vulnerable now — knowing Kane was out there, probably waiting for me — than I had even when he had me strapped down. Then, I hadn't known I should be afraid of him. Now, I knew — and I was.

"We'll figure something out."

I could tell by the look on his face he was worried, though. He didn't look at me, but concentrated on the sparse traffic and whatever was going through his own mind.

"I'll have to go back eventually. Find some clothes."

"Jimmy can take you shopping."

"Is he my babysitter now?"

At that, Gabe did look at me. "Yes."

I frowned, but his mild, no-nonsense expression didn't change. "As long as you're at the house, you'll be safe. If you need to go anywhere, for any reason, you will go with Jimmy or myself. Is that understood?"

I nodded. One part of one percent of me wanted to protest I didn't need their protection. The part of me that had let Kane chain me sat very still and shaking, ready to agree with anything Gabe said.

"Understood, Sir." I stared at my hands in my lap. I wasn't afraid. Gabe wasn't keeping me captive. He was protecting me. I wanted to be protected. The destruction in my house only drove home how Kane felt, how wrong I'd been about him.

Gabe didn't say anything about my calling him Sir and a little piece of me found that comforting.

Gabe

Sir.

I should have corrected him. He shouldn't be calling me that. I wasn't the Dom he thought he needed. I wasn't sure he *needed* a Dom at all. He should have a friend, and I had a vague hope maybe he could find that in Jimmy. I certainly wasn't up to being the objective presence he needed in his life right now. The fact my old friend had agreed to come back to the house with us gave me hope he wanted to help Rory at least a little bit. Maybe he just wanted to protect me from myself, but either way, his presence would be good for my new charge.

I glanced over to see Rory chewing on his lower lip and alternately examining his twined fingers and looking out the passenger window. He looked tired. Frail and scared. Hell, in his position, most people would be freaking out. I hoped it was a good sign he could sit there quietly and not be hyperventilating or fuming. I didn't know him well enough to know for sure, though. I wished I knew someone I could call, someone who *did* know him well enough, but he hadn't mentioned anyone. In fact, he'd been conspicuously quiet on the subjects of friends and family, raising my suspicions that he either didn't have any, or had fallen out with them. Many people did, when they came out. Just being gay was too much for many families to accept. Being gay and being a submissive to the *nth* degree, as he so obviously was, could be more than a lot of people would understand.

And if he was friendless in the world, that only hardened my resolve to teach him how to get his submissiveness under control. He had to know how to get along without compromising who he was, just as much as he had to learn how to recognise a safe Dom and learn how to conduct himself inside the Community. I had my work cut out for me.

When we arrived home, he went straight to the kitchen.

"I'll make us lunch," he announced, opening the fridge and rooting through it.

"I can order something, Rory."

"Please." He straightened and turned, watching me over the refrigerator door. "I have to do something useful, if that's all right with you." He closed the door, set down the juice jug, and walked over to me. "Unless you have something you'd prefer me to do…"

His lashes fluttered demurely on his pale cheeks, and he licked his lips. He wasn't so innocent he didn't know how to seduce, that was for sure. With his hands clasped quietly in front of him, he exuded an air of sensual submission that had my cock jumping and my head spinning.

I was, in fact, reaching for him when the back door crashed open and Jimmy came bouncing in.

Rory practically jumped into my arms, his entire body shaking and quivering, his hands gripping tight wads of my shirt and a little bit of my skin on one side.

"Ah! Shit!" I cringed away, grabbing the offending hand and holding it away from me.

His reaction was immediate and damning. He crumpled, falling to the floor on his knees, his head down, his hand limp in my grasp. His whispered apologies wavered through the kitchen between pants.

I dropped his hand. "Rory —"

"I'm so sorry!" He didn't look up. His voice was plea enough.

Jimmy and I exchanged a look and he took a hasty step back. "I'm sorry, Gabe. I didn't mean —"

I cut Jimmy off with a wave of my hand, aware just the sound of his deep voice made Rory cringe more. This was something that went way deeper than Rory's recent and relatively short association with Kane.

"Rory." I waited until he raised a tentative face. "Go up to your room and wait for me, please."

He nodded and didn't quite bolt up the stairs.

"Jesus, Gabe. I didn't think."

"No." I ran a hand through my hair. "Not your fault. He's stressed already. But that…" I shook my head. "That was more than Kane."

Jimmy nodded his agreement. He had personal experience with the kind of trauma that would cause that kind of reaction.

"Someone used to beat that kid," Jimmy muttered, his voice low and angry.

A few long, steadying breaths later, I looked up to find Jimmy watching me shrewdly.

"You're going up?" he asked.

"I have to, don't I? Have to calm him down."

His bearing changed ever so slightly. The relaxed, easy set of his shoulders stiffened, his spine drew him up an additional few inches. It was his belligerent, tough stance he pulled out when he absolutely could not bring himself to bow to my command. "You should let me."

I probably should have. But visions of Rory's terrified face, the memory of his trashed house, the scars and bruises, the dark, cavernous need in his eyes — they all conspired to break me down. I'd resisted about as much as I could have. The overwhelming need to bring him peace, to see him smile happily, to feel safe, if just for a moment, wasn't something I could deny any longer.

"Gabby, this is the real deal. I hope you know that."

I met Jimmy's eye and found he'd retreated. Not physically, but the bit of him that could submit to me bending him over my desk had gone.

"You either let me go up there now, Gabby, or you commit. He can't take anything less."

And neither would Jimmy. He didn't have to say the words. I could see it in his bearing. This was his ultimatum, and he had every right to issue it, after everything we'd been through over the years.

I nodded, turned, and headed for the stairs. Behind me, the back door opened and closed quietly, but it felt final like none of the times Jimmy had stormed out on me ever had. When I didn't pause to examine how I felt about that, I knew I was doing the right thing.

Jimmy

Damn. Damn, damn, and damn.

The little shit had called it right, and I should have argued. I should have stood up for myself and told him no, I wasn't in any way interested in what Gabe did.

"Fuck me."

The bike ride that took me through town and into the shopping district only got me almost killed three times. It hurt to know Gabe was upstairs coddling Rory and not chastising me for driving like a maniac. It shouldn't.

Damn, damn, and fuck.

Just because I didn't *want* to be in love with Gabriel fucking Stark didn't mean I wasn't. Just because I wanted to hate the little prick he loved instead of me didn't mean I could.

I parked at the corner coffee shop, grabbed a brew, and wandered the shops. I knew Gabe wouldn't think of it, so I picked up a couple of shirts, a pair of jeans, and some socks and boxers in Rory's size. Itty bitty, skinny little fucker size.

Quickly stuffing the purchases into my saddle bags, I wheeled around and headed back to the Alley. Not to Gabe's, though. I didn't think I would want to set foot in that house for a while.

Instead, I went to Peter's Diner and took a stool at the end of the counter. I was glad the place was almost empty. It would fill up soon, but right now, I needed this particular stool to be empty. It was my stool, and when I picked it, Peter knew what I wanted.

"Boy," Peter greeted me quietly.

I let out a breath of relief, straightened up before he told me to, and tried a smile. "Sorry I had to call Adam in on his day off."

"Was it about the guy Gabe took home last night?" His voice stayed low, but there was an edge to it.

I tried not to let it get to me.

"Yeah."

"That why you're here?"

This time, I did drop my gaze to the countertop. It was all the answer he needed.

"This is about the guy Gabe took home last night, too."

He waited for my answer, which I refused to give him out loud. Bad enough I had bought the jerk clothes and couldn't hate him. I didn't have to admit I felt like a less-than-worthy cast-off.

"You know this isn't how we work. We'll call you when we want you."

I figured that was what he'd say, but I had to give it a shot anyway. "I'm sorry. I thought maybe—"

"You're a good boy, Jimmy. Come back when Adam gets home."

I looked up, once again hopeful. "Thank you."

"Don't expect us to go easy on you because your heart is breaking, boy. We expect service, and you'll give it."

"Yes, Sir."

I got up to leave, but he stopped me with a hand on my wrist. His fingers dug in, and he held me in place, speaking over my gasp.

"I mean it, Jimmy. This isn't a pity fest."

"No, Sir." Just his firm touch was getting to me, and I had a hard time catching my breath. I'm sure he could see my hard-on through my eyes, because his face softened.

"You came to us. You'll act accordingly."

"Yes, Sir."

"Wait here."

I sat back down without a word. Peter disappeared into the back. I heard the heavy door that led to his and

Adam's upstairs apartment thump closed. A few minutes later, it thumped again and he was back. He sauntered through the break in the counter to stand behind me. I didn't dare move.

"You have the rest of the day." Something dropped onto my collarbone and drew snugly around my throat. "When Adam calls, I'll let you know where to meet him. You will present yourself, and if he feels like accepting, you can come home with him."

"Yes." I had to swallow my nerves behind that tight collar. "Yes, Sir."

"Good boy." He patted my shoulder and kissed the top of my head. "Off you go."

Obviously, my nerves and my desolation were all over me, because Peter never collared me. I couldn't stand it. He knew that. But he thought I needed it. Who was I to argue? He could own me for a night. No one owned me forever. Maybe that's why Gabe wanted Rory and not me.

"And Jimmy?" he called when I was at the door.

"Yes, Sir?"

"Drive carefully, please."

He knew me. "Yes, Sir."

Chapter Five

Gabe

Rory's door was open, and Rory crouched, a small figure on his knees, curled down around himself in the middle of the floor.

I knocked softly on the open door.

A tinny, distant voice told me to come in. It didn't sound like him at all.

"Rory."

No response. Just shivering, a mat of dark hair covering his face and his arms so tightly held his muscles strained. I couldn't begin to imagine what he thought I would do.

"Rory."

A convulsive shudder shook his thin frame. Sleep deprivation, malnourishment, and now emotional stress had finally done him in. If he wanted to, he couldn't respond to me. He had nothing left.

I went to him, took him by the arms, and gently pressured him to uncurl. "Look at me, Rory."

He did, but there was nothing in his eyes. Just blank fear.

"I'm going to help you. You're going to do exactly as I tell you."

He nodded. It was painful to watch. This wasn't surrender or submission. Just blind desperation, and it killed me to have to use it to get him to cooperate, but until I had him calmer, feeling safer, it was all I had to work with.

"Stand up now."

He did. Slowly.

I moved around him, not wanting to frighten him, but not wanting to tower over him either. The bed would serve as a decent place to sit.

I patted the mattress beside me. "Come sit."

Silent, he came and settled where I indicated, moving like he expected me to strike him at any moment.

"Tell me who hurt you?"

His dark eyes opened on me, swallowing me.

"Kane." He sounded so hollow.

"Before that."

I could see there was an answer. He shook his head.

"Tell me, Rory."

"Doesn't matter. He's gone."

"Gone?"

A long time he sat, picking his nails and staying silent. I'd already given him the rule about telling me the truth. It was up to him to follow it or not. I hoped to hell he would because the last thing I wanted to do when he was in this state was punish him in any way.

"My first place I got when I moved away from home was a room," he said at last. "In this college house. I was younger than everyone. Smaller. The guy who owned the lease, he...gave me a break on the rent." He whispered the last bit and didn't elaborate, but his meaning was clear enough in the way he kept his focus firmly on the floor and his hands tight in his lap. "It wasn't that bad. But some — sometimes, he just...lashed out. It wasn't really his fault —"

"Rory —"

"No!" He jumped up and faced me, hands tight fists, arms ramrod straight at his side. "Don't! It wasn't his fault. He was schizophrenic. We didn't know. He didn't know. Not when it first started. I never knew till after I moved out and someone told me he killed himself. Sometimes, I still just...get jumpy. For a while after I moved out, he...kind of...stalked me."

He closed his eyes. His hands went slack, and he shuffled forward. Just a few steps, and one hand came up towards me.

I took it.

He didn't say when, exactly, that had been, but obviously if he'd been younger than college students, he'd been just a kid. Extrapolating, he must have moved out at an early age, which was just further proof that he couldn't rely on his family since he'd felt the need to leave them.

"You know Jimmy would never hurt you."

He nodded. "It didn't matter who it was for a minute, I was just back there. I couldn't think. I didn't mean to hurt you."

"It was a pinch. It surprised me. It was nothing."

"Okay." He curled his fingers around mine at last and shuffled closer. "I should apologise to Jimmy."

"Ah. Later."

"Okay."

I waited. There was more he wanted to say. His gaze darted around my face, and he took the last few steps that put him nose to nose with me.

"Hold me?"

"Sure."

He was so soft, despite the too-prominent bones. Soft and pliable and needy. I wrapped an arm around his shoulders.

"Jimmy has gone for now, Rory. It's just us in the house. Are you okay with that?"

He nodded against my chest. A whisper of words I couldn't hear brushed against my throat as he lifted his face, and the next thing I knew, he was kissing me.

Being caught off guard was the flimsiest of excuses for accepting that kiss. Feeling his hips rise and his hard cock pressing against me was no reason to let it continue. Hearing him moan, feeling the vibration of it in my mouth wasn't a good reason to deepen it or bury my fingers in his hair and hold him there while I plundered his mouth.

We both had to breathe eventually.

"Want you," Rory whispered, his lips still touching mine. "Please, please, please."

A tiny pull on his hair to tip his face up met with no resistance. His eyes glowed when he looked at me, shimmering from their dark depths with lust, with certainty, and excitement.

I nodded. "Get undressed. Come to my bathroom."

He nodded, his tongue darting over his swollen lips. "'Kay."

"The proper response would actually be—"

"Yes, Sir."

"Much better."

When he arrived a few minutes later, and watched the water pour noisily into the tub, his face had gone a little pale.

"Something wrong?"

He just shook his head and pushed a hank of hair off his face.

When I thought there was enough warm water to make it comfortable, I stripped and climbed in, held out my hand to him. "Come on. You too."

"You want me to scrub your back?" he asked. His voice was husky over whatever was making him hesitate, but he managed a weak smile. He didn't hide that he had gone soft in the intervening minutes, likely under the influence of second thoughts.

"I want you to sit here." I indicated the space between my legs as I let my knees fall open against the sides of the tub. "I want you to get warm and I want to talk."

"Talk." His hand slid into mine — encouraging, although he still didn't step over the lip to join me.

"We must, Rory."

"I have to tell you everything."

Good. That I didn't have to explain it — again — was also encouraging. I nodded. "The first thing I want to know is what you think will happen when you do tell me what's bothering you."

His eyes went big, too bright, and his fingers tightened painfully around mine. "You'll…"

"I'll?" I lifted one eyebrow, using the expression deliberately to catch his notice. "You know how I will react, do you?"

His head wagged from side to side, almost comic in his vehemence. "No, Sir."

"Of course you don't. Try again. Tell me what *you think* might happen if I know the whole truth of Rory Sanders."

"May I sit down?"

I couldn't help but smile. I'd been afraid he was too unsettled to take my offer. That he wanted to join me — even if it was a not very well veiled ploy to sit with his back to me and hide his face when he answered my question—filled me with relief.

"You may. But you will still tell me everything."

He just nodded and made his delicate way into the tub to settle in front of me. He kept a chunk of space between us. His back and shoulders remained erect, and his buttocks, tight and small, fitted neatly between my raised knees so that he didn't have to touch me. It was a small enough concession to allow him his space for the time being. I let my gaze travel over the marks still visible on his flesh. The swelling had gone down, at least, even if the lines of red remained vibrant against his porcelain skin. The thin, open gashes were scabbed over, and I made a mental note to rub some cream over them later. I'd noticed the layers of bruising around his hips and bottom, but thankfully, they had disappeared under the water. I wanted to touch, trail a soothing caress over his shoulders, where he wasn't marked, but he'd as good as requested space, and I had to respect that.

After a long minute, he pulled his knees up, wrapped his arms around his shins, and rested his chin on his knees. "I'm afraid if I tell you what happened, everything that happened, you'll think I'm a complete idiot."

"That's a valid fear, given what you've been through, but I would appreciate it if you gave me the benefit of the doubt and not lump me in with the men who hurt you."

He nodded, barely lifting his head from his knees. "That's fair."

"Thank you."

"I met Kane...four months ago, I think. About."

That still surprised me. As far as we'd been able to tell, Kane hadn't associated with any of his victims longer than a few weeks. It only confirmed, as if I didn't already have enough evidence, that Rory was special to Kane in some way. All the more reason to protect him.

His story was pretty much what I'd expected. Kane spent most of his time with Rory keeping him bound and dependant on his goodwill. Goodwill which he doled out in distant and miniscule dribs and drabs. Keeping my anger in check as Rory spoke was the most difficult thing I'd ever done.

"I almost never — I couldn't — " His shoulders shook, and he lowered his head until his forehead touched his knees. A few deep breaths and a lot of shaking later, he lifted his head, reached to turn off the trickling water, and shifted his weight. Very tentatively, he let some of that weight settle towards the side of the tub. His arm rested against my leg, and he let out a little puff of breath. "He was never satisfied, even when I followed his directions to the letter. Nothing was good enough for him."

I carefully shifted until my hand cupped the arm leaning on my leg. He didn't pull away. I noticed the shift in his wording — a shift that moved the blame for the damage off Rory's shoulders and placed it squarely on Kane's where it belonged. I wondered if he had done it on purpose or if it had been unconscious.

"I'm a good person," he told me — as though I needed to be told, but I let him talk. "And I can be a good sub if — if you gave me the chance. You're not like him." As he spoke, his body relaxed into the warm water, into me, and I took his weight without otherwise touching. Not yet. Not until he gave me permission. "You like me the way I am. Even when I freak out. I'm not afraid of you." His head came to rest on my shoulder, and he twisted slightly, settled to where he could nuzzle against my neck. "You haven't once tried to tell me I had to be different than I am."

In a minute, his nuzzling and cuddling was going to cause me to show obvious effects against his backside. I was only human, and my body was hardly immune to his charms.

"There is a lot you can learn, if you want to," I told him. "A lot of things I think it would be good for you to know, but only if you want."

"I want." He snuggled, squirmed, and deliberately pressed himself against my hard-on. "I want to be safe."

"You don't have to seduce me to gain my protection. You already have that."

"Can I just seduce you because, even if you weren't a Dom and I wasn't a submissive, you would still tick off everything on my list of hot and want?"

He was almost on his side by now, and he dropped a hand between my legs. It was tempting to let him have his way with me. Oh so tempting.

"That's very flattering, and I'm glad I do that for you." I took hold of his wrist and pulled his hand away from his goal. "But I *am* a Dom, you are a submissive, and if this is what you want, you will accept it on the right terms."

I felt the unmistakable tension ripple through him, but this time he didn't look down. He let me see the trepidation in his eyes, and it only served to make me want him more.

"First, a kiss, then I want you turn around and rest your back against me."

I should not have found it adorable the way he tilted his face up, yielding to the faintest pressure of my fingers under his chin. His eyes drifted closed, and I took a moment to admire the dark lashes against pale skin and savour the hard, wild beat of my heart. The realist in me knew I was putting us both in a lot of very real emotional danger, but the rewards…

His kiss was tender, almost sweet, but very real. I expected to feel his need and his uncertainty. Instead, his kiss tasted of deep desire and complete surrender and trust. It went straight to my head via my heart. I was lost.

I had to follow through, though, so I pulled myself out of his sweet grip with my fingers twined in his hair and waited until he opened his eyes. There was the nervousness I had expected. I waited until he'd focused, his attention solely on me.

"Now I want you to turn around, rest against me. And keep your eyes open."

"Yes, Sir."

The low, throaty response shot fire through me, and I rocked slightly, rubbing my cock against his flesh, showing him what he did to me.

He didn't turn away quite quick enough to hide a tiny, excited grin.

"Cheeky."

He ducked his head, but before worry could lodge in him, I wrapped an arm around his chest, pulled him back tight against me. "Yes, Rory. You do that to me. Don't doubt I want you. Never doubt that. Now do as I've told you. Get comfortable and open your eyes."

He nodded, settled back, and although it took him a few heartbeats, he did finally lift his face and open those bottomless black eyes to look in the mirrored wall at the end of the tub. After another second, he drifted his fingers shakily over my forearm clenched across his chest. "That looks good there." His head tilted to one side. "I'm very pale. Skinny."

"Pale is good. Skinny we'll fix. Now lift your knees and spread your legs."

Perfectly obedient, he positioned himself as requested and watched me in the mirror.

"Are you nervous? You're shaking."

He nodded. Honest. That was good.

"No need to be. There is nothing ahead but pleasure for you, Rory." I kissed the side of his neck as I moved my hand and wrapped my fingers firmly around his erection. He was long, thin, perfect in my grasp, and his lips fell into a parted, panting pout as I began to move.

Rory

I didn't understand the order to keep my eyes open. It was all so much easier when I could close them. I could trust his touch—it spoke of his care and patience—and with my eyes closed, I didn't have to worry I might see disappointment on his face. Easier to enjoy everything if I couldn't see how seriously he was taking this.

He didn't take his gaze off mine, didn't afford me the freedom to look away. His hands on me were firm, comforting and constricting all at once. It was so hard to know which sensation was truth. If I wanted out, would he let me? But his fist wrapped around my cock felt so damn good, and his lips teasing along my neck spread heat through my entire body. I hadn't lied about him hitting all my buttons. His broad, muscled build, slightly greying-around-the-edges hair, and penetrating eyes were everything that physically did it for me. His strength and control made my knees weak. Not a very manly reaction, but an honest one.

"Are you watching?"

Gabe's voice in my ear drew me back to the sensations he was giving my body. I nodded. Through the clear water I could watch his hand slowly move up and down my cock. It was a double shock of bliss to see his thumb glide over the tip and to feel it. My hips jerked on their own. I gasped.

Gabe clamped his arm tighter around my chest, holding me still. "Let me." He brushed his lips over my ear.

It was impossible not to melt into him, not to give him the control he sought. The vague disquiet at being held immobile against his body eased as his fist moved over my cock and his words of comfort and approval sent shivers down inside to where I lived. My head dropped back, my eyes dropped closed.

All movement stopped.

"Rory." The flat, hard command sifted through the instant tension.

"Rory." Softer, this time, though no less commanding. "Open your eyes. I want you to see how lovely orgasm looks on your face."

I made myself refocus on my own reflection. "Lovely?"

"Hot, then." He grinned, brushed my ear again with his lips.

"How do you know it would be lovely? You've never —" He started moving his hand again, and I gasped at the firm, hard strokes. "Seen —" I managed before Gabe's fingers found my nipple, his teeth the side of my neck, and my balls tightened. "Ahhh!"

"I have now," he whispered.

Aftershocks coursed through me as I came down and he only held me more firmly.

"And I was right. You orgasming is possibly the sexiest thing I've ever seen."

"What about you?" Unease, unwelcome, but impossible to ignore or banish, wiggled up through the lethargy. This was where the telling point was. "You haven't."

"Shhh. Just relax."

"But…" I wanted to do what I was meant to. I was supposed to satisfy him, not the other way round. What was I going to owe him if I didn't do what I was meant to do? When was he going to collect, and how?

The stress of waiting for him to change his mind squeezed out the pleasant lassitude. My back began to ache under tight muscles, and a shiver ran up my spine. The more I tried to hold it off, the tenser I became.

"Shhhh." Gabe smoothed a calloused hand over my stomach. His fingers played in my hair.

"Just tell me what you want. I'll do it."

"This is what I want."

I felt a little pressure on my hair, looked up to see in the mirror that he had his lips pressed to my head and he was watching me, concern in his pale eyes.

"Just this, Rory. Nothing else."

"You—you haven't got off."

He smiled, turned me until I was curled between his legs, my hip pressed against his groin. I could still feel his half-hard cock. A finger under my chin lifted my face, and I looked up into his.

"This is not about me, Rory." He bent, took my mouth, tender, but deep, possessive.

I couldn't resist giving him every ounce of my attention. His tongue inside my mouth, his hands, one glancing over my chest, the other in my hair at the back of my head, held me to him as surely as if I was bound. The difference was, if I pulled back, I could get away. He gave me that freedom. Then he assured me, through every touch and word, every taste and caress, that I didn't need it.

When he finally let me go, he'd taken the tension and uncertainty with him. I remained curled against him, my cheek pressed to his chest where I could hear his heart beating rhythmically, heavy, synchronised to his steady, deep breathing.

I lifted a hand, laid it on Gabe's chest, daring to touch, feeling the tremors of fear snake through me despite his constant reassurances.

"You're okay, Rory." Gabe touched his lips to my hair again, his hand came to rest on mine. "You're okay. This is good." He moved, pulling me closer and wrapping an arm around me, then a leg, the weight holding me warm and secure within the bath's steamy comfort.

He made it so easy to relax. The trouble was remembering he was not Kane. I was not going to be made to pay for letting my guard down. I had to believe that. I couldn't survive another Kane in my life.

"Gabe?"

"Yeah."

"I might fall asleep. I might…" *Let myself trust you.*

"It's okay. You've had a long weekend. You should sleep."

A few minutes more we lay there, until the bath lost some of its heat. I drifted, floating under the light waves and his limbs. It was heaven, letting go, feeling like as long as I floated there, he would never let me come to harm.

He did give me a soft shake after a while.

"Rory. We should move this to someplace more comfortable."

I nodded, reluctant to lift my head, to move from under his comforting weight.

"Come on, lo—"

His chest heaved as he drew in a deep, almost shuddering breath, and I was suddenly, instantly alert. His rough hand drifted a light, skimming touch over my shoulder, down my arm, and he sighed.

"Wake up, love. The bath is getting cold."

Love?

I pushed myself upright to see his face, but he didn't look at me. "I'm awake."

"There's a robe on the back of the door. Put it on and go to my room."

"Yes, Sir." Maybe I'd misheard through the fuzziness of exhaustion.

Gabe

I watched him climb slowly, carefully out of the tub. He showed all the signs of physical exhaustion and emotional numbness I expected. Mentally, I kicked myself. I'd meant to give him release, hoped it would relieve some of the humming tension he'd been carrying just under the surface. Tension I'm sure he had no idea had him wound so tight. He'd probably been living with it for months until it became normal.

And it had worked. Better, even, than I'd hoped. He'd almost fallen asleep in my arms. I couldn't have planned it better. Until I used the 'L' word, and he'd tensed right back up.

Normally, I would have had him drain the tub and tidy the room, but he was dead on his feet, even if he didn't recognise it. I quickly did the work myself and went to the bedroom.

He was sitting, perched, really, on the edge of the bed, and he jumped to his feet the second I entered the room. The robe puddled slightly at his feet, too long for him, and I realised that he really was quite a bit smaller than me. He pulled the fluffy terrycloth tighter at his throat.

"Cold?"

He nodded, eyes fixed on the shaggy yellow rug under his feet. I watched his toes wiggle in the deep, plush pile and smiled.

"Well, then." I went over, gently removed his hands from their clutching grip on the robe, and undid the hard knot he'd tied in the belt.

He finally looked up at me as I began rubbing my hands firmly over his arms, then carefully over his abused back and the rest of him.

"Dry off," I told him, doing it for him while he stood there, stiff, uncertain. "And get on the bed. On your stomach. I'll rub the cream on your back. Then under the warm blankets with you." I hoped I could get him into the bed before the tension completely returned. His muscles were still soft, pliable from the warm water, and I turned him around, kneading his shoulders a bit before finally slipping the robe off.

I didn't give him a chance to stand there shivering, wondering, but prodded him towards the bed. "Go on. Get in."

After a hesitant, silent moment, he whispered, "Yes, Sir," again and climbed up onto the mattress.

"There you go."

Except he didn't lie down. He turned around to face me, sitting, waiting, hands clasped in his lap.

"Lie down, Rory."

Finally, his big, dark eyes lifted, and he looked at me. "You're not—"

"No." I reached over to run fingers down his cheek as his eyes went darker, worried. "I have some work to do, and you need to sleep. Lie down so I can do your back."

There was no mistaking his glance downward, and no way I could hide my engorged cock.

The worry in his eyes deepened.

"That's my job," he pointed out, his voice low and resigned.

"Not right now." I stepped forward, realising he was not going to respond to the gentle touches. He didn't recognise what was happening. How Kane had made him forget what tenderness was in just four months…

"Rory, you're no good to me in this state. I would appreciate it if you would stop trying to control the situation. Your only job, as of your concession down in the kitchen, is to do what I tell you to do. Understand?"

He nodded. Dropped his chin to his chest. I was about to order him to lie down, close his eyes, when his shoulders shook. He actually sniffled.

"I'm sorry. Sir. I tried to tell you. I'm no good—"

"Stop." It was impossible not to pull him into an embrace, to hold him, reassure him he was wanted. "Rory, you are good and wonderful. You're also exhausted and frightened and out of your depth. You haven't disappointed me in any way. Please trust me. Trust what I'm saying. I know what's good for you right now."

His head bobbed against my chest. "I'm trying."

"Good. Then baby steps, yeah?" Pulling him away, I lifted his face to look into his eyes. "Baby steps, and right now, the only step you're up for is to lie down and get some rest."

He nodded, his eyes still watery, and I kissed him, just a quick, gentle peck.

"Lie down."

He did, and I took my time spreading the cream over his back. Once I was done and he'd rolled onto his side to look at me, I couldn't help the urge to smooth his hair back, cover him up.

"I'm not a child."

"No. Indulge me. You're gorgeous. I just want to look after you, make sure you're comfortable."

"I am."

"Okay. I'll be back to check on you soon. Stay in bed. I want you to rest."

"I will."

By the time I dressed and made it to the door, he was asleep. I breathed out a sigh of relief.

Chapter Six

Rory

"Breathe, Rory. Breathe."

My fingers tightened into fists. A tiny whimper bled past my lips.

Gabe's hand pressured me, firm between my shoulder blades. My arms pulled back, captured by the cuffs holding me. I didn't want them, couldn't pull free, and I hated it.

"Breathe, baby."

This time, the whimper sounded more like a sob. I tried to tell him. I couldn't get the words out.

"Do as I say." Gabe's voice lost the soothing, husky rasp, smoothed out, refined. "Do it, or I'll be forced to take measures."

Take measures.

"Please." I was trying. I'd told him I was. Why was he tying me down?

"Please what?" Kane's voice broke over me like shards of glass. "Too late for please, slave."

The whip lash from that dream woke me, sweating and cringing, surrounded by Gabe's scent, comfortable and safe in his bed. I pulled the covers back over me, but once I was awake, I didn't want to be there alone, waiting on his pleasure.

I snorted. *You just want to be where he is*, I chided myself.

"So what?" It wasn't so bad, being where he was. He was kind. And there was nothing wrong with answering myself back, either.

I pushed back into his pillow and closed my eyes. He'd said to stay, to wait. I'd wait. My determination didn't keep the nightmares away, though. Every time a dream started with Gabe and ended with Kane, I woke shaking, miserable.

When Gabe came to me, when he decided I was ready, would our play turn to torture because I couldn't get my mind back from Kane? I didn't know how to escape the man when he was there, always in my head telling me I'd failed—again.

Finally, too exhausted to go around the circular argument with myself, I drifted off again.

I pulled in another desperate breath. Great whipcords of tension lashed through me. I couldn't relax. Every time Kane told me to, it only made it worse until I shook in the bonds and couldn't keep my whimpers and pleas to myself. I waited for the lash, and the wait was worse than the pain.

All I had was a disembodied voice, taunting me, belittling me, and the cuffs holding me in place. There was no escape from that voice, from everything it said and all it meant. I was captive. I would always be captive.

I curled in on myself as much as the bonds would let me. It wasn't much. Wrists and ankles were held by rigid leather and heavy chains, keeping my legs apart and my body stretched awkwardly. I couldn't find a comfortable balance that didn't leave me exposed and too vulnerable, hanging painfully from muscles not meant to support my full weight. I knew the dreams weren't really dreams. Just memories I could only fight while I was awake.

Kane had only reserved this position for special occasions. Those times when I'd completely failed and his usual whipping punishment wasn't good enough. It didn't matter how I braced myself. When he fucked me, it hurt. He wanted it to. And he hardly ever topped one time. He just went on and on, shared his 'toy' with people whose faces I never even saw. That had happened only twice, but twice was two times too many.

Just being strapped into this position was enough to plunge me into panic. All the thrashing in the world would not stop it, only make it worse, but hanging there, passively taking it was beyond me.

I woke again, the sobs still spilling out, Gabe's bed in a shambles, the covers kicked half to the floor and sweat coating my body.

Nothing ever stopped the nightmares.

Shaking so that I couldn't even walk a straight line, I stumbled over the thick shag to the rough, pale carpeting beneath. My legs collapsed once, my knees sliding along the short pile and coming away stinging and skinned. I had to heave in breath after breath before I could climb to my feet using the door frame to pull me up.

"Pull your shit together. He'll never keep you like this. It's just a dream."

As if that mattered. Even a dream was real when you were in it, and who's to say giving myself to Gabe, however well-meaning the guy might be, wouldn't just plunge me back into the nightmare?

In the bathroom, the faint residue of the fragrant bath remained in the air. It sank into my brain, permeated the terror, and this time, the deep breath didn't burn against too-tight muscles. I looked in the mirror over the sink at my long hair — almost ponytail long, in fact — and held it back with one hand while I splashed water over my face with the other.

When I looked again, I resembled something of a drowned rat. I knew Gabe wouldn't approve of my getting out of bed, much less appearing in his presence looking like something the cat dragged in. But I needed him, so I straightened, squared my shoulders, made myself presentable as possible.

The nightmares were mine to deal with. I could be Gabe's. I could do it. I just had to keep the black dreams to myself. He had enough to worry about, and if he didn't know about them, it would be easier for him to show me what I needed to know. Then I could use what he taught me to keep the dreams under control. I just had to convince him I was okay, that he could show me.

I took my time, showered, gritted my teeth at the residual sting of water on the raw skin of my back as I washed my hair. I used a bit of the cream Gina had given me to spread over the rug burns on my knees. The marks on my back still stung, and I wished I could reach to soothe those, too, but I would have to ask Gabe for his help.

That's when I realised my clothes were gone.

"Fine. If this is the kind of slave he wants..."

Ruthlessly, I shoved my reservations aside. I'd just ask him where they were and if I could have them back. He'd never discouraged questions. I'd just confront him, tell him I wasn't comfortable walking around with nothing on. He'd give me back my clothes.

But instead of marching down the stairs, I tiptoed back to his room and curled up on the bed because it was too frightening to contemplate the idea he might refuse.

A long time passed in which I knew I should be sleeping, but the dreams were too fresh and my worry too acute. I hated that my experiences with Kane were infecting everything in my life. That he had violated my home and my conscience and destroyed so much of my *self* made me furious. I clung to that. Fury was easier to deal with than fear I couldn't move through.

It was also exhausting. I drifted again after a while, not quite asleep, because I watched a sliver of light track across the floor as the sun moved just outside the curtains. That reminded me it was the middle of the day. Sun bright and shining out there, and all I wanted was to stay right where I was. I pictured standing in my yard, the bright morning bouncing off Gabe's salt-and-pepper hair, turning the silver a shimmering, precious hue, and my mind wandered to how I could portray that on paper.

Which only reminded me my studio was trashed, the tools of my livelihood destroyed, and I wasn't sure I had enough savings to replace the equipment it had taken me years of careful scraping by to accumulate. Once the cops were done with it, I would have to go back and clean it all up. Before we'd left the wreckage to come back here, I'd overheard Gabe say something to Jimmy about builders, and I wondered just how much destruction there was. Did home insurance cover this sort of thing?

I realised I was letting out one deep sigh after another, and forced my mind off it all. Tomorrow was Monday. I'd borrow Gabe's phone and call my publisher. She'd maybe be able to advance me something to replace some of what

I'd lost. I wondered what I'd tell her had happened. Not the whole truth, because that was just too humiliating. A break-in, then. She'd work something out for me – I hoped. I was just glad I'd sent her the latest batch of work on Friday before going out. At least I had nothing I had to replace for the current book, and she would forward me any copies I needed to get back on track.

Still thinking about work and figuring out how I was actually going to be able to do it, I at last slept a little more, my last coherent thought that Gabe was a decent guy and I was a grown man. He fucking well would give me my clothes back.

Later. When I had more energy, I'd go find him and ask.

Gabe

My own feelings aside, I knew Rory was going to be more work than I was used to. He was just that much more damaged than any sub I'd yet taken on, Jimmy included.

Although, Jimmy was a different animal altogether. He had never really healed completely from all the abuse he'd endured in his life. He'd only learned how to live with it. I was never the guy who was going to make Jimmy put it aside and really trust.

Thinking back over the tempest that had been my months with the big man, the relationship that had developed when I realised he was not just any guy looking for a job at Rolly's, it hurt all over again. I'd gotten too close, wanted too badly to fix him. His leaving – it had been necessary for him, but it had killed me. I took too long to get over him, and I guess, really, I never completely had. I'd never fully let him go, and that, obviously, had been bad for both of us.

I hoped he'd left for good this time. Not because I didn't want him around, but because I knew I was holding him back from finding what he needed. That wasn't me. I was just clinging to a dream of something we'd never had. Maybe I'd been hanging onto to the idea I could still fix him; if I could just figure out how.

I sighed, flopped into my desk chair, and brooded. I had to let go. I was no good to Rory while still burning a torch for Jimmy, however pointless. And if I was honest, I had to admit my feelings were all about me and not really about Jimmy at all.

"God." I thumped my elbows painfully against the desk top as I leant forward and dropped my head into my hands. "Get the fuck over yourself." I had no guarantee that once Rory was straightened out he'd stay either. I had to make sure he didn't know how I felt. He had to be free to choose to leave, but more important, he had to *feel* free to leave when the time came, or I would tie him up in the same sort of knots I'd done Jimmy. Not fair to any of us.

"This is pointless."

I straightened, snatched up the phone, and dialled. I had work to do. I needed first to talk to my old friend, Peter, and find out if his cop partner, Adam, knew anything that could help me. If Adam couldn't share what he knew, Peter might know something. He had his ear to the ground in just about every fetish bar in and out of the Alley. He's the one who had brought Jimmy to my attention it the first place, hearing he'd been wandering the clubs looking for any Dom who'd use him, and not caring how badly he was hurt. Peter had put a quick stop to that, and a lot of fucked-up individuals were put on notice they were not welcome in the Community because of it.

I called the diner first, but Skate, the most recent addition to the staff, told me his boss had taken the rest of the weekend off. Before I could thank him and hang up, though, he blurted out a string of questions.

"It happened again? That fucked-up shit, he did it again? Why hasn't anyone stopped him? He left someone at Rolly's. Marky, he isn't in danger, is he?"

I sighed. I didn't bother to ask how he knew. He found out a lot of things I wouldn't expect to be common knowledge. I didn't know how, but he'd been useful on more than a few cases and all he asked in return for his information was the safety our little Community offered him.

Skate was a decent kid. He'd come to Rainbow Alley shortly after Marky, following his fellow gang-banger to warn him some of their "brothers" were gunning for Marky. The story, as I understood it, was that Marky and Skate's little brother had been lovers and had conspired to leave the gang. But at the last minute, the little shit lover had changed his mind, sold Marky out, and gotten himself killed in the process.

Why Skate chose to warn Marky he was in danger instead of shoot him himself, as he must have been ordered to do, I never fully understood. But he'd stuck around, got a job with Peter and a room at Dean's, and now he volunteered at the youth centre for gay teens. Not that he was gay himself, but it was good to have people there who weren't. People who represented "the other side", as Skate put it, to show those kids there were straight people who accepted them.

"You don't think if we could have stopped him by now, we would have?" I snapped.

"Sorry." He sounded contrite, but his voice still had an edge.

"Marky is fine," I reassured him. "You know Rolly's not going to let anything happen to him."

"I know. Still, I worry. I mean…"

He trailed off, but I kind of understood where he was coming from. Unless you could put yourself in that headspace, understanding the D/s dynamic was next to impossible.

"I know. But you have to trust Marky, too. He's with Rolly. And even if he wasn't, he wouldn't go do anything stupid. He fully understands how it works. Kane preys on guys who don't. Like the kids you counsel. In fact, you should talk to Jimmy. Get together with him and see if you can find a way to broach the subject with them. They should know the dangers."

"Sure." He sounded a little sceptical.

"I mean it. They should be on their guard, and it might help you understand."

Our little Community, dubbed Rainbow Alley some years ago after one of the first gay bars to open in the city, was a small, interlaced and tightly knit place. It was no secret Skate and Marky had drifted apart because of Marky's relationship with Rolly, and Skate's inability to fathom why Marky gave the older man so much control. It was also no secret they both missed each other.

"I'll call Jimmy," he promised.

I hoped he would, for everyone's sake. I was serious about giving those kids as many tools to safely navigate the minefield of queer life as we had to offer. And I did want Marky and Skate to mend their friendship. It would give Jimmy something to concentrate on, too. That last was probably more to mollify my own guilt, I knew, but it couldn't hurt.

I hung up from that call and dialled Peter's home number. He answered on the first ring. His partner, Adam, picked up as he was greeting me.

"We figured you'd call a lot sooner," Adam's deep voice purred over the line, and I smiled. He was a good guy, good cop. I knew he'd help if I asked.

"I would have. But I had to sort a few things..."

"Jimmy told us." Peter's voice was a lot harder.

Judgement. One Dom to another. One *disapproving* Dom to another. He and Adam had taken Jimmy in after my screw-up, gotten him back on his feet, taught him to live with who he was rather than try to fix him.

I didn't have a word to say to his reprimand.

"We're coming over," Adam said at last, subdued but firm.

Peter hung up.

"Adam."

"I know, Gabby. You just have to be careful. Jimmy wouldn't have said anything if he wasn't worried about you both. He even went shopping, if you believe that. Picked up a few things for Rory. I'll bring them."

"Rory's different."

"Yeah. Jimmy said that too. Just hang tight. We'll be there in a few."

He hung up, and I was left feeling at once relieved and apprehensive.

Peter was not about to sit back and let me fuck up another vulnerable man just to ease my own conscience. Trouble was, I might have actually lost sight of where my conscience stopped and my heart took over. I might have lost sight of everything but what I wanted. I needed Peter to tell me I was doing the right thing for Rory, and I was terrified he'd say I wasn't.

Part of being a good Dom was knowing yourself and I knew I wanted something more. I'd been looking for something deeper for a long time now. A willing sub to train or a mutually satisfying way to get my rocks off just wasn't enough anymore. I wanted what Rolly and Marky had, what Peter and Adam had. I wanted something safe and permanent in my life. I wanted a life, and it was hard not to imagine Rory had dropped into my lap at just the right moment to take it. He wasn't ready. I *knew* he wasn't ready, but I wasn't sure I was man enough not to try for him anyway.

This morning was a good example. I should not have gone so far with him. I should have let Jimmy look after him. It had worked out. I think. But my rationale told me I was moving too fast, that he wasn't ready. He was beautiful and needy and lost. He needed me.

"No, Gabriel. You want him. Not the same thing at all."

I sighed. Talking to myself was a bad sign.

I took out my case file again to study the marks left by Kane's whip. They showed up so beautifully on his pale skin. No doubt that's part of the reason Kane had chosen him. It wasn't about a relationship, or even about dominating him. It was about marking him, claiming him in some way Rory might never be able to forget. It was a territorial, obsessive, dangerous need to own.

Disgusted, I shoved the pictures of Rory's back and ass to the bottom of the pile and looked again at the photo of his face. He had more colour now than when the picture had been taken, but the shaggy, unkempt look remained. He was losing himself inside the creature Kane wanted to create. I had to make sure he never lost sight of who he was.

I touched Rory's picture, as though I could caress him by running my fingers over the glossy print. There was something there. Something beyond the need and fear looking back through the camera lens. There was a man in those black eyes that was worth the effort.

The roar of motorcycles hauled me from contemplation of that beautiful, haunted face. I tucked the photos and folder safely back under lock and key in the desk drawer. He didn't need to see it now, when the marks were almost gone. I wanted him to feel good about himself in every way, and the quickest, easiest way to start was to show him his own beauty and encourage him to maintain it. I double-checked the drawer was locked before lifting the edge of the blinds.

A smile eased some of the tension. Adam and Peter might not bring anything new to Rory's case, but I had faith Adam could find out more than I could, and that once he understood the man I was trying to help, he'd do so. Peter was my oldest friend. Whatever advice he gave, whether I liked it or not, I would heed it. He had a disinterested view of the situation. I could trust him. They were already coming in the back door when I reached the kitchen.

"Hey." Adam's bass voice rumbled up from his barrel chest, and Peter gave a little shiver. It made me smile to see they still affected one another that way.

"Hi." I clapped Adam on the shoulder, gave Peter a nod, and brought the water jug and glasses to the table. "Please tell me you can give me some clue as to who this Kane asshole is. Tell me we can catch him. Put him away."

Adam unzipped his heavy leather coat in silence to reveal his bare, hairy chest and the thick studded collar he always wore off duty. He went in for the flashier displays of Peter's ownership when he could, and I had to say, he wore it well. He waited, and once Peter had sprawled his endless legs under my kitchen table. Adam poured three glasses of water, set Peter's in front of him, then mine, and picked up his own glass. After Peter sipped, so did he.

"Thanks, Adam."

The big man's bright smile went a long way to lifting some of my dark mood. I glanced to Peter, waiting for his slight nod before offering Adam a seat.

He grinned at me and folded his mountainous frame onto one of my kitchen chairs. It seemed small and frail under him. He settled so that one knee rested against Peter's thigh. Peter laid a possessive hand on Adam's knee.

Maybe I was just hyper sensitive to the nuances today, but it seemed they were more…touchy than usual. Maybe Rory's plight, and Kane's influence, was having an even deeper effect on the Community than I'd first thought.

"So? Do you have good news?"

The instant Adam shifted, glanced at Peter, I knew he wasn't going to tell me what I wanted to hear. I shouldn't have been surprised. Kane had left half a dozen men bound and helpless in public clubs without ever leaving a description, or even a hair or a fingerprint behind. The only account we had from any of the more lucid victims was of a long-haired man who wore makeup like a mask. On any given night, that could describe half of the fetish community out for a good time or a hook-up. He'd been careful, and he was not going to make a mistake now. If he'd even been in Rory's house — and there was nothing to suggest it had been him except gut instinct — he would not have left any evidence of it.

"You have to understand something, Gabe," Adam began, "it isn't like we have guys breaking down doors volunteering to stake out fetish clubs. We can't cover all of them at once. That leaves us with hit and miss, and you can pretty much guarantee he has some way of knowing where we are and when."

"How?"

"How should I know?"

Peter squeezed his knee, and Adam bit his lip.

"Sorry." He pulled in a breath. "I'm sorry. It's so damn frustrating. Like we aren't people. Don't matter. Even if I came out—" He shook his head. "Being a cop isn't enough to make them see. The only way I keep the position I have, the only way I can help, is to pretend I'm someone they approve of. And even that is on shaky ground lately. The more I look into this Kane asshole's doing, the more I get sideways looks and muttering about being a homo lover." He heaved backwards in his chair, making it groan, and crossed his arms over his broad chest. "Bunch of uneducated ape-shit fuck-ups."

"Those are your colleagues, darlin'," Peter reminded him.

Adam just made a face and looked away from us both, his expression dark and scowling.

"I'm sorry, Adam." It didn't help that he was so torn between the job he loved, the man he had to pretend to be on the outside, and who actually he was. "So." I tried, gently, to bring the conversation back around to why they were here. "So far, all we have is miss."

Adam sighed heavily again, rubbed a hand over the back of his neck, and loosened his defensive position some. "I'm afraid so. Kane is lying low. Unless Rory can give us a better description than we have so far, we haven't any more to go on than we did before."

And Rory's description wasn't much better than anyone else's, despite his longer association with the man. Kane never showed his face without the makeup, and Rory described his face paint as something to rival a KISS wannabe. Or he'd covered Rory's face, and I clearly remembered the shiver that ran through Rory when he told me about the times Kane reserved for the blindfold.

"He's lying low," I said at last. I knew he was. He wanted Rory back. There was no chance of him making a mistake. He wanted his prize and he would bide his time until he got what he wanted. Trouble was, I didn't know how to draw him out.

Peter sat up a little straighter. "I've been thinking about this. He didn't leave Rory like that for no reason. I don't know what, but I would guess he was trying to teach him something. Break him. He had every intention of coming back for him. If not at the club, then at his house. Why trash it?"

"Because he was pissed he didn't get what he was there for?" I guessed.

Peter glanced at Adam, who nodded. "I saw the pictures of the bed. He cannot be allowed to get his hands on Rory again. He'll try, and if he does, whatever he's done to the man so far will seem like a cake walk. The asshole is unbalanced and now he's angry."

I nodded, mulling over what Peter had said. "He didn't come back to the club for him. He left him in the last room, the one Gina always saves for the end. She doesn't like it in there, and she waits until Jackson, the DJ, has finished his own clean-up. He usually helps her."

"Is that common knowledge?" Adam asked.

I shrugged. "Among the staff, probably. They're a pretty tight-knit bunch."

"Then someone had to pass that information on to Kane."

"Rolly picks his staff very carefully, Adam. You know that."

"I'm not for a minute saying anyone passed it on deliberately, with any intention of hurting anyone. All it takes is a conversation. One comment."

I found it hard to believe someone on Rolly's staff would have talked to Kane and not known what kind of person they were talking to. I said as much, but Peter and Adam exchanged glances.

"What?" I said.

"The thing about the kind of man who repeatedly does this sort of thing is that he has to be approachable, doesn't he? He has to gain these men's trust before he can get the shackles on. By the time they figure out what Kane really is, it's too late."

"Think about it." Peter leant forward. "He had Rory believing in him for months."

"He had Rory scared half out of his mind. He's still scared." In fact, given what he'd told me of his past, he'd been scared before he ever met Kane, maybe before he stepped foot out of his parents' house.

"What we need," Adam said, half to himself, "is to draw Kane out. Lure him somehow." He glanced between us, the shrewd cop superseding the submissive lover. "Give him bait he can't refuse."

"No." My reaction was immediate and visceral. "No."

Adam raised a hand. "Hear me out."

"I won't—"

"You don't even know what I'm going to say." Adam's face clouded. "It's a good idea."

With some effort, I closed my mouth and let him talk.

"Let's assume we're onto something about Kane trying to teach Rory a twisted lesson of some sort." His face took on a disgusted squint. He didn't have to wax poetic about what any of us thought of a Dom who'd leave his submissive chained and defenceless in a public place. "If,"

Adam continued, glossing with some difficulty over the revolt we were all feeling, "he intended to retrieve him at any point after the club closed, he never had the chance. Rory's been safely tucked away here for the duration. A couple days with no sign of his property will have Kane pissed. If he's smart, he'll be running for the hills, but on the off chance he's still looking for an opportunity to get Rory back..."

"No." There was no way they were ever going to talk me into what I thought Adam was leading up to. I recalled what amounted to the artistry of the lash marks on Rory's back. A man didn't do that and not want to see the results of his handiwork. Maybe he'd planned to find Rory at his home and nurse him back to acceptance of their relationship. I guessed he'd used that method in the past from the way Rory tended to turn docile at the slightest hint of kindness. I had no idea what this sick bastard thought he was creating, but there was no doubt in my mind Rory was the canvas. That there was any will left when I looked into Rory's dark eyes was enough to tell me Kane wasn't finished, wouldn't be finished, until Rory was completely broken. It wasn't too late to remind Rory who he was, what he wanted for himself. I'd be damned if I'd give Kane even the chance to finish what he'd started.

I took a deep breath, attempting to settle the sick feeling in my gut, the need to run upstairs and make sure Rory was still sleeping in my bed. Just to see his face, peaceful as I'd left him—safe.

"Kane started something," I told them, extrapolating from what I knew and projecting to what I thought a man like that might be thinking. "He'll see it through. He'll go through a lot to see it through." But what if Kane couldn't get his hands on Rory? Would he start over on someone else? I couldn't imagine him leaving his work half finished. I couldn't imagine it because I knew how I felt about Rory. I would never let him go without doing everything I could to heal him. In some ways, Kane and I were not that different, and that thought terrified me.

When I looked up, Peter was watching me, and I know he saw the realisation in my eyes.

"Rory is in danger as long as Kane is out there somewhere," Peter said.

And not just from Kane himself. Rory was in danger of being swallowed whole by his need to be dominated and my need to protect him. The danger of him losing himself was as great either way.

Peter leant forward, his leather pants creaking, his boots scraping across the floor. He touched my hand, drawing my attention. "The surest, quickest way to eliminate the greatest threat is to get this Kane person to come to us, Gabe. You can see that. And the best way to decide how we are going to do that is to let Rory make a few of these decisions on his own. He deserves that much consideration, doesn't he?"

I nodded. He was right, and I hated it, because it meant Rory wouldn't be safe. "You want to use him as bait." I shook my head as I pulled out from under Peter's touch and glare, looking to Adam. "You're a cop. How can you even contemplate using a civilian like that?"

It was Adam's turn to lean forward, putting himself solidly in my space, all cop and all business. "I'm also a submissive. Maybe you don't get it, and if you don't then what the hell you've been doing all these years, I have no idea. The amount of trust it takes to let someone –" He glanced at Peter, who nodded. "When we enter a scene, Peter is everything. You know this. Everything he does, he does for a reason, whether I know what that reason is or not. I have to trust that. I put everything on the line, and

Peter has the power to destroy me. He chooses not to." A grin flashed across his face. "He uses his power for good."

We all chuckled, but Adam turned back to his point quickly. "Rory put everything on the line and he lost it all. You don't know what he wants now. You don't know what kind of anger he has under all that fear. Frankly, I'd be shocked if he didn't jump at the chance to find Kane and make him answer a few questions. I'd be more worried that once he's a little more balanced, he'll go off on his own and try, and where are you then? Kane loose, Rory gone. How will you protect him? You can't protect him from what's inside himself, Gabe. You can only hurt him by denying it exists."

"Like I did with Jimmy." *And Collin.*

Peter touched his lover, and Adam sat back without answering me. He didn't have to. It wasn't like any of that was news to me. Sometimes, though, it was easy to lose sight of the other person's perspective. Adam just wanted to make sure that wasn't happening here.

"If Kane gets at Rory again without someone there to help him, he could do a lot of damage," Adam pointed out unnecessarily.

"He already has," I muttered, furious and wishing I could slap Adam down. But he was only speaking from the vantage point of a man who regularly put everything he was in the hands of another and trusted that person to protect him when he was helpless. For a cop to have found the strength to give up that much control spoke volumes about him. Punishing him for speaking the truth just because I didn't want to hear it would say a lot about me.

I glanced over, and Peter was watching me, his glare sharp and protective. "You understand where I'm coming from," I said, pleading. I knew he did. He might look like he was sitting there, casual, in a friend's kitchen, but his expression said he'd go against anyone, even his oldest, best friend, to protect the man who trusted him above all others.

He nodded. "I also understand the kind of dangerous ground you're treading with Rory, Gabe."

He was all tense muscles under his relaxed pose, every inch the Dom, and my hackles rose.

I waited, watching him. I'd known him all my life, trusted him, loved him like a brother, and now I was ready to order him out of my house. No one had the right to tell me how to deal with my own sub.

"Shit." I slumped back in my chair. That was it. He *was* mine. I was fooling myself if I thought I could keep a separation, and Peter knew it. He'd seen me travel this road before—with Jimmy, with Collin—and he didn't trust me to keep my perspective, to keep Rory's best interests at heart. I hoped he was wrong.

Adam glanced between us. "What just happened?"

"Find another way, Adam. Please."

The big cop glanced between us again, spent a long minute watching me, watching his partner. At last, he shook his head. "I suppose I could do it."

Peter's loose posture lost all hint of casualness.

I picked up my glass of water, drained it, and set it down. Peter watched me as I nudged the glass towards Adam. After a protracted moment, Peter nodded. Adam reacted like he'd been released from stasis. He got up, refilled my glass, and set it back in front of me.

I sighed. "No, Adam. You can't."

"Why?"

"You're too well trained."

"I've gone undercover before. I know how to turn off the cop."

I smiled. "I've seen it. I know. But that isn't the training I was referring to."

Peter looked up at him from his chair, a stern look that had Adam dropping his gaze to the table top. He hunkered down in his seat so as not to be towering over us. A second later, his face flushed.

"Oh."

Peter broke into a grin, sat up, and bumped his chin, getting him to look up. "Don't worry. It looks good on ya, babe."

Adam only flushed deeper, but also looked pleased with himself. Contented.

What I wouldn't give to see that look on Rory's face. It only proved we were right, though, and I nudged their attention off each other and back to the problem at hand. "So what other options do we have?"

"The only option is to draw him out, get him under control."

A tiny squeak of a sound from the doorway at my back shifted all our attention there.

I caught a flash of wide, horrified eyes, flying black hair, and too much pale skin. A fast glimpse of Rory's ass, a bare foot, and he was gone, pounding back up the stairs. A second later, a door slammed.

"Fuck."

"That's our cue." Peter tapped Adam on the shoulder. "Come on."

Adam stood, zipped up his coat. "I'll be in touch once I've got the full police reports."

"Thanks." They were almost out the door when it occurred to me to make sure Rory saw them leave. "Can you wait in the drive? Just want to make sure he knows you're both gone."

Peter nodded, and Adam left. "Promise me something, Gabe."

"What?"

"If you're not sure, about anything, call me. Ask. Let me be your perspective."

"I can manage."

"I don't want to see you go through that again, what happened with Jimmy. You both survived, but he's tough. After Collin, you're just bastard enough to have survived that, too. But the rest of us, we don't like to see you like that. Please. You have friends."

I nodded. I had friends like Jimmy. Friends who didn't need me screwing up their lives again. Friends who would never forgive me if I didn't let them make that choice for themselves.

"Thanks." I managed a smile and told him to watch the spare room window.

Chapter Seven

Rory

The sound of footsteps stopped just outside my door, and I watched the handle. That little hook and eye would not stop him if he really wanted to get in, but I hoped it was enough to send a message he would heed. My body. My choice, submissive or not. I was done being anyone's plaything.

"Rory?"

"Go away!"

"You know it doesn't work like that, Rory."

"I'm not coming out! You three can play amongst yourselves." My heart hammered. A week ago, I never would have dared. I would never defy Kane. Not even now, but Gabe... He might make me pay for it later. But he might not.

"Rory!" Gabe's voice cut across my thoughts, and I realised I was pacing.

"No!"

"Open this door."

I stopped, stared at the blank wood. "You'll have to break it down. I'm not coming out!"

"Look out your window, then." His voice still held the timbre of command but none of the sharpness, and I wondered if maybe I'd imagined the anger.

"Why?" It didn't hurt to ask.

"Just do as I say."

It couldn't hurt, could it? I moved to the wall beside the window and peered between the blinds. In the drive below, both men I'd seen in the kitchen sat astride big Harleys, helmets in place. The skinny one lifted a hand in the general direction of my window, revved his motor, and rolled out of the drive. With just a quick glance up, the bigger man followed. In seconds, they'd disappeared down the street.

"Okay?" Gabe asked from the other side of the door. He didn't wait for my humiliated response. "I'll leave clothes here by the door. Apparently, Jimmy went shopping for you. You can come to the kitchen and help with dinner when you're ready."

His footsteps padded away.

I waited about ten minutes, until I heard pots clanging and the sounds of chopping and cooking from below, and until I was chilly enough to overcome my embarrassment. The clothes he'd left outside my door were nice—good quality, well fitting and modest. Just jeans and a T-shirt, but respectable. I'm not sure what I expected. Feeling ten times a fool, I could not force the blush from my face as I presented myself in the doorway of the kitchen a second time.

Gabe glanced up, knife stilling as he examined me, head to foot. "Good." He resumed chopping, the knife moving fast and furious along the unfortunate carrot. "You look nice."

Not a word about my freaking out and insulting his guests.

"Where's Jimmy? Is he home yet?"

"He's gone to stay with friends. I don't expect him back."

"Oh."

He glanced at me. "That a problem?"

"No!" I smiled, though it felt a little stretched, and the way his lips turned down, I could tell he knew it. "Can you tell him thanks for the clothes? They fit nice."

"They do." Then after a minute, "You'll need to shave to go with them, but that can wait until after supper." He nodded towards the sink. "Wash those potatoes, please."

"Yes, Sir."

The silence in the room fell somewhere between taut and dangerous. He must have had questions he wanted to ask about my overblown reaction, but he didn't. Which was a relief, because I had answers I wasn't sure I wanted to give.

"I'm sorry I didn't shave. I couldn't find a razor."

I felt his eyes on me and knew I was being measured. After a few minutes, he set his knife down and pulled something from his jeans pocket. He set it on the counter between us. It was a key.

When I glanced at him, he nodded at it, popped a carrot into his mouth, chewed and swallowed. "That'll open most of the locked cabinets in the house. A drawer in each bathroom, you'll find razors and over-the-counter drugs. Aspirin, cough syrup. Usual stuff, but I know what's there. You need anything, you ask." He tapped a finger against the drawer front near his hip. "Knives are in here."

I continued to wash the potatoes, but I noticed the gold, circular key hole on the drawer.

"It won't get you into my desk, the liquor cabinet or beer fridge, or open anything in the garage, so don't bother."

I had to wonder why he felt the need to keep so much of his everyday life under lock and key.

"Some of the men who come here," he said, as though he'd read my mind, "they come from bad places, aren't as strong as you. It's my job to protect them. Even from themselves, if need be."

"You thought I was suicidal?" The thought shocked me. I'd had a shitty few months, but that had never even entered my mind.

"I had no way of knowing." He set the knife down again, turned and leaned on the counter to face me. "I learned the hard way that some men cannot live with the idea they are submissive. They'd rather be anything else. Even dead."

"How do you help someone like that?" It was morbid to ask, and I kicked myself the second it was past my lips.

Abruptly, Gabe turned back to the carrots, picked up his knife, and chopped feverishly. I figured he wasn't going to answer me when he spoke.

"I couldn't. A guy who really wants to be dead will get dead, one way or another."

"I'm sorry."

"Me too."

Those two pained words closed the subject. Some things were just none of a guy's business.

Quiet invaded the tense space around us, softening it some. The vigorous chopping slowed and finally stopped. I guessed from the pile on the chopping board we'd be eating leftover carrots for a while, but Gabe seemed calmer. The gentle gurgle of water disappearing down the sink was almost soothing once he'd stopped, and I risked a tiny peek over.

He still had his head down, mincing garlic. I'd noticed in the bath that he wasn't overly muscled, but he wasn't small, either. He was cut and fit, and the tight T-shirt he had on accentuated every curve and bulge of his biceps as he moved. It skimmed over the flat expanse of chest and abs. I remembered the light dusting of hair, the sensation of strength when he'd held me close. Safe.

I bit my lip, brought my attention back to my task.

"Something wrong?" he asked.

I dropped the slippery potato I'd been scrubbing and spent the next few seconds chasing it around the sink. "No." I caught it and held tight. "Just thinking."

"About?"

How could I possibly tell him I'd been thinking about snuggling against him for security, like a little kid? Except the thoughts that came after had nothing child-like in them at all. I couldn't tell him he was sexy, comforting, just about everything I'd ever wanted, right there in one package, chopping vegetables like a normal person.

This wasn't a relationship. He'd made that pretty clear from the start. I was here until they figured out what to do about Kane. Until they were sure I was safe. I was here to learn, but not to fall in love. I didn't really have any illusions on that score. As nice as he'd been, he was training me. He had no interest in me beyond an interesting challenge and quite likely a healthy dose of pity.

"Nothing," I said at last.

His knife snicked softly against the countertop as he set it down. His hand was hot on the small of my back as he reached past me and turned off the tap. Tension ripped through me, coiled around every muscle, whitening my knuckles on the unassuming potato.

I'd said the wrong thing. As he turned me to face him, fear rose up from somewhere about my knees, making everything in its path wobbly and uncertain.

"I can't help you if you lie to me." His hands withdrew, leaving me even more unsteady. He took the potato out of my hands.

I stared at my damp, empty fingers.

"Look at me." Just one finger under my chin lifted my head.

His eyes were clear, showing only calm interest. No anger. No derision.

"Tell me what you were thinking about."

He left me little choice. When he made a command in that voice, I had to respond and he knew it.

"Just..." I waved a flopping hand in his direction. Lord, where had my nerve gone that I couldn't even tell a guy he looked good? "I like that shirt. On you." I realised I'd dropped my gaze to his chest and lifted it to meet his eyes, which were filled with amusement but not judgement. "Suits you," I said softly, encouraged that he hadn't laughed in my face. I wavered a bit, found I wanted to lean into him, and decided to risk touching him. I pressed a hand to his chest. "I was thinking about how nice it was. In the bath. When you..." I had to take a breath, but his fingers caressed my cheek and I smiled. "Felt good to be held," I admitted.

"Rory."

I would have looked back up at his face again. Seemed I couldn't keep my eyes off the rise and fall of his chest, but he yanked me forward, and I stumbled into his embrace.

"Was that so hard?" he asked after a minute.

"Yes," I grumbled, but he only squeezed me a bit harder.

"I know. But you did it."

"I did."

"And thank you. I'm glad you like my outfit."

I hadn't even gotten to the way his ass looked, but I figured a quick caress, maybe a little squeeze would show my appreciation. Pressed against his chest, I was feeling less and less shy about appreciating him a lot more.

"Hey." Both hands on my biceps, he pushed me away and looked into my eyes. "We're making supper."

"Uh…"

"Uh?"

"Supper. Yes, Sir."

He gave a little nod, a slight smile, and released me. "Good. Finish the potatoes. I'll get the meat on the barbeque." At the door, tray of steaks and utensils in hand, he stopped and caught my attention. "Maybe after."

The way his voice dropped, what he'd said sounded like a promise, and my heart skipped. Suddenly the idea of scrubbing and mashing potatoes, sitting across the table from Gabe, seemed like the best thing in the world. It seemed normal. Not just safe, but normal. And if he told me after to clean up and go to bed without sex, I would. Because no matter how I screwed up, he kept giving me another chance, explaining, calming me like I was a spooked wild thing. Maybe, in some ways, I was. And the fact that was okay with him made it easier to let him tame me.

Gabe

Steak was the last thing on my mind with the feel of Rory's fingers digging into my ass still fresh. Not even Jimmy, bold as he was, would dare make such a blatant move on me. But then, Jimmy had been a chained creature out of the gate. I got the impression Rory had a lot of experience with guys under his belt before he'd decided to explore his submissive side. He already knew what he liked in bed, what he wanted in a guy, and that had nothing to do with being submissive. All I had to do was get past the tight, grating sensation of the jealousy *that* caused to see it as a good thing.

Jimmy had never had that sort of freedom and would never want it now. Which made him more vulnerable than he wanted to admit. In the beginning, he'd clung to any Dom who'd take him. Although he knew better now, his inexperience had been backed by a sadistically abusive family who had broken him in ways I wasn't sure he would ever really get over. Now, he stuck to the very few men who'd been good to him: me, Peter—when he and Adam wanted a third—and Rolly, before Marky had entered the picture.

"Not your problem now, is it, champ?" I shook my head at the turn of my thoughts but that didn't stop me arguing with myself as I scrubbed black goo off the grill. "It's better this way."

He was getting too comfortable waiting for me to call, knowing I would eventually. High time he found his own life. He'd never go out and get his own guy if he clung to me.

Which didn't give me the right to basically kick him out and leave him on his own without some support. But he was strong now like he hadn't been when I met him, even if he did still have cracks and crutches. He would find a way to get by. Hadn't he already done so? Peter had said they'd talked.

Which turned my mind to thoughts of Peter indulging in his favourite form of domination—watching Adam and Jimmy together. It wasn't exactly a bad mental picture, but it didn't help to imagine that when I was already teetering on the brink of self-doubt. Rory couldn't afford for me to doubt my abilities now.

The disagreeable scent of char pulled me back to my task, and I glared down at the grill. A bit of old fat I'd failed to scrape away in my preoccupation smoked, and I flicked it aside. Drawing on all the Zen concentration I could find, I focused my attention back on my job and waited for the grill to be hot enough to accept the slabs of meat. Enticing Rory to eat then sleep was my only priority tonight. It would help if the cow was cooked to perfection, or at least not charred to ash.

By the time I'd carried the rested meat back inside, the kitchen was full of delicious smells. I found Rory had only cooked half the carrots I'd chopped in my frenzy. The rest, he pointed out, were safely washed and stowed for another meal. The table was set, complete with candles, which inexplicably made my heart thrum a bit, and he was stirring some fragrant concoction of butter and herbs over a low flame.

"For the steamed carrots. I know it's not particularly heart-friendly, but…" He watched me worriedly.

"It smells fantastic."

"I steamed the carrots, so if you want me to just eat them plain—" He cut himself off by nipping his bottom lip, turning soft red flesh white with the pressure. One hand played nervously over his belly, bringing attention to his too-slim waist.

I leaned over the pot, drew in a good whiff of the sauce. "Did you come up with this recipe?"

He shook his head. "My mom's. Best cooked carrots I ever ate were at her table. She showed me a lot of what I know about cooking before…" He paused, took a breath. "She died when I was seventeen. Breast cancer…" There was something sinister about the dark edges that invaded his eyes when he trailed off again. Another story he wasn't ready to tell.

"If this is something you love to eat, Rory, I'm pleased you chose to share it with me. I'll get plates."

"Already did." He pointed shyly to a pair of clunky clay plates, almost platters they were so big, sitting on the counter, each with a small, prettily arranged bit of greens on them.

I touched the edge of one plate, a flash of memory stabbing through me. They'd been a gift from Collin, made by his own hands. Imperfect, but that only made me love the gift more. I noticed Rory had dug out the small bowls that went with the plates. He was filling them with carrots and sauce and placing one on each plate. I watched in silence.

His hands were so steady, small but sure as he dished out a mound of aromatic mashed potatoes for each of us. The steaks were next, and those he laid out and topped with a sauté of mushrooms he'd had stashed in the oven. The final effect was a meal that not only smelled delicious, but looked like something off the food network.

"You got a lot done in twenty minutes."

"It's all in the timing. Besides, all the hard prep was already done, and anything's easy with a well-stocked fridge and pantry. I'm glad I'm not the only one who likes to cook." He popped a carrot in his mouth and grinned.

It brought a smile to my face, reminded me he was not Collin. Whatever flashes of fear Rory's trauma created, at his core he was a strong, happy man, and he wanted to be again.

"No, actually, you aren't, but from the smells, I'm going to have to concede the floor. I'm competent with the grill and the chilli pot, but beyond that, I just hope the fresh, good quality of the ingredients is enough to mask my amateur skills."

Rory set both plates on the table and waited for me to take a seat. "Good. Then I have something to teach you in return for your help."

I sat, motioned him to do the same. "Not that I require any sort of recompense from you, but I won't turn down a few cooking lessons."

Rory nodded. Once he was seated, fork in hand, he still waited for me to start. "I guess it will be good if you learn, since you'll be addicted to good food, and eventually, I guess I might not be here to prepare it for you."

Our eyes met over the candles and food. I could read it in his eyes. He wanted me to tell him he wasn't going anywhere. I wanted to say it. I wondered if he saw that. But he didn't ask, and I didn't say it. It was too soon. I hoped my not agreeing with him on that point was enough for him for now and wished it was enough for me.

When he smiled, a soft, openly hopeful expression, and returned his attention to his plate, I breathed a sigh of relief.

One day at a time.

We ate in near silence. He didn't eat even half his steak and potatoes, but he did polish off the carrots and salad and drank two glasses of water. When he sat back and gave his plate a tiny push away, I looked up.

"That will go well with some eggs in the morning," he said, watching me, waiting for my reaction.

I nodded. "There's fresh fruit and frozen yogurt for you to snack on later." It wasn't a suggestion.

"Yes, Sir."

I let the half-eaten meal go. It was an issue. We both knew it, but I could hardly force-feed him. He had to work his mind around the unpleasant memories himself. All I could do was remain positive when it came up and reassure him I knew he was capable of making his own decisions on the matter.

"Can I ask you something?" His question came over dishes, his hands elbow deep in sudsy water.

"You can ask."

"Thank you, Sir."

I waited. He washed another plate, a glass, set it in the drainer, but didn't remove his hand. The water in the sink rippled in outward rings around his other wrist.

"Go ahead, Rory. Ask."

"Am I...physically unattractive to you? Is that why you don't want to, why it's just professional?"

How was I supposed to keep my distance when he asked that? I couldn't lie to him. I demanded truth from him and he deserved as much from me. I picked up his hand from the glass, pulled him from the sink, and turned him to face me. "In all honesty, Rory, you could have walked out of my wet dreams. Physically, that's just icing." I stroked his hair, watching the way it curled around my fingers, like every part of him longed to cling and keep me close, and God help me, I wanted that.

"What does that mean?" He didn't sound plaintive. He sounded firm, sure he deserved a clear answer that made sense.

"It means if I built the man of my dreams, he'd be you." There. I waited, watching his face, hoping that pronouncement wouldn't send him running, or make him fall into my arms. He needed to stand on his own first.

"I see." He extracted himself from my grip and turned back to the sink.

The rest of the dishes were done in silence. When the last plate was stashed on its shelf, he turned to me again.

"I don't understand you, Sir." When I opened my mouth to speak, he actually held up a hand. "But I don't have to understand. I know you want what's best for me, and obviously you don't want to get hurt. So I have to trust you. I do trust you."

"That's good."

"You said once that I had to know my limits, had to know what I wanted before I gave myself to a Dom. That he should listen to what I want. That it was about more than just protecting me."

"I did. It is."

He lifted his face, bit his lip in that way that made my cock twitch almost violently, and swallowed hard.

"Then I want you to stop treating me like a victim. I made mistakes. Bad things happened. I know you're not Kane. I know what I want." He glanced around the kitchen. "I walked in here and it felt like I'd walked out of a dream, like I finally woke up. I'm not afraid of Kane. I'm not even afraid of the bad moments, the memories I know will happen, but mostly, I'm not afraid of you. I'm a grown man and I need you to treat me like one."

I didn't tell him I was afraid of Kane enough for both of us. He didn't need this new confidence undermined. Instead, I smiled and touched his face, because he was, I was beginning to understand, a very tactile person. All the more monstrous if Kane had figured that out too, and used it against him. A bigger miracle that he hadn't lost the instinct for it yet. The way he turned slightly, into my touch, told me it was still very important to him.

"If you truly think you're ready for this, and everything it means—"

"I am."

"Then you will refrain from interrupting me again, for one thing."

He clamped his lips shut and blushed.

"What it means is that for the duration of time you live in this house, you belong to me. You follow my rules, you serve me, and I will make sure nothing happens to you and that you have everything you need."

When I stopped talking, he nodded.

"Good."

He smiled a pleased little smile, but there was still something he wanted to say. I could see it in his eyes. He didn't open his mouth, though.

"Tonight, I want you to actually sleep, Rory. You've had a gruelling few days.

"Yes, Sir."

"There's something else. What is it?"

"It's about earlier. I behaved badly today. If you think it would be appropriate, I would like to apologise to your friends. My freak-out chased them off, and I'd be grateful if you would let me make it up. Please."

"You'll get a chance to talk to them."

More chance than I would have wanted, knowing what they would be talking about. I just wished this was the start of a true training, a chance to focus solely on him and what he needed. Until Kane was dealt with, that just wasn't an option.

"Now." I took another opportunity to touch his hair, soft, springy curls once again trying to entrap my fingers. "Upstairs and into bed. Wait for me."

"Your bed, Sir?" He sounded surprised but not distressed.

"Is that a problem?"

"No, Sir." He flashed another of his brilliant smiles.

I'd only seen a few of those, but it was my intention to draw them out as often as possible. He was beautiful, lit up from within that way.

Before I went up, I stopped in the study, picked up the phone, and called Peter.

"When you met Adam," I said, cutting off his greeting, "was it—"

"Instant."

"It isn't about wanting to fuck him. Or even wanting to protect him, though both those things are true."

"You want me to tell you you're doing the right thing."

"Am I?"

"Gabriel, sometimes you second-guess yourself into a tailspin no one can pull you out of. How many men have you helped? You have this extraordinary gift, being able to figure out what other people need and finding a way of making sure they find it."

I sighed. "It's just what being a Dom is about. I—"

"No, Gabe. It isn't. I mean it is, but you seem to think it comes as easily to everyone as it comes to you, and it doesn't. I know what Adam needs because we spend a lot of time talking about it. It isn't instinct for me to be able to put my own pleasure aside in favour of his. It's a skill I learned," he chuckled, "like giving good head. Because it makes him so happy to be in that headspace, I figured out how to give that to him. I spent a long time with him getting it right, learning him, realising how much he needs it and how much I enjoy doing that for him. You? You just look into a guy's eyes and know where to take him. That's something special."

I wasn't really sure he had any idea what he was talking about, but he hadn't answered my question. "So why does it always lead back to one thing with Rory?"

"What thing?"

"I don't ever want him to leave."

Peter chuckled.

"How is that funny?"

"It isn't. I'm sorry."

"Jimmy...Collin... I knew they would move on. I thought...but I always knew I couldn't keep them. I wanted to help them. But it wasn't forever." I let out a deep sigh. "Not like this."

"Not like love," Peter said softly.

"I thought love was supposed to be this great, illuminating moment when everything got simple."

"It is."

For a full minute I sat with the phone in my hand while Peter waited.

"Gabby."

"Yeah."

"Stop thinking. Go upstairs and look at him. Tell me it isn't the simplest thing you've ever known."

"I thought you'd be against this. It sounded today like you were."

"I'm against you trying to create something that doesn't exist. You've tried that before and it doesn't work. It hurts everyone."

"Is Jimmy—"

"He's fine."

"Tell him—"

"Let him come round on his own, yeah?"

"Yeah." That hurt. Knowing I'd done him harm undermined everything I wanted to believe about myself.

"Gabe. He's fine. You aren't responsible for how he feels. Trying to give him something you don't have to give is no good for either of you, and watching you fall for someone else... It's hard for him, but he'll get around it. He's tough."

"I shouldn't have asked him to help."

"No, you shouldn't have, but in all fairness, he hasn't been as forthcoming as he should have about his own feelings, and you couldn't know you'd crash hard for Rory in less than twenty-four hours."

"Fuck. I screwed up."

"Everyone does occasionally, Gabby. But Jimmy's here. He's safe, and we won't let him go getting all self-destructive. Not that he's showing any inclination to go back to bad habits, but just so your mind is at ease. He's in good hands."

"Thanks, Peter."

"You're welcome. Now concentrate on the matter at hand."

"Rory."

"Do us all a favour, Gabe. Let yourself just feel what you feel. Put all that responsibility and shit on hold for two minutes. Look into his eyes, and you'll see what everyone else has already seen."

I didn't know what to say to that, and when I said nothing, Peter let out another exasperated sigh.

"Not to put too fine a point on it, but you say his name and get a look. Anyone else says anything, and you bristle like the overprotective bear you are. I have every intention of avoiding being in the same room with both of you if at all possible. The doe-eyed sappiness could contaminate even my good sense."

"Funny."

"But true. Most very strange and unexpected things are. I'm hanging up now."

I nodded, not even thinking he wouldn't see it. The dial tone buzzed in my ear after a minute, and I hung up the receiver. I had Peter's blessing. I don't know why it mattered. Maybe because he'd been my friend and seriously into the scene as long as I'd known him. Before he'd met Adam, he'd taken great care to be good to his subs, and his perspective, his opinion, mattered to me.

His advice seemed sound. With some effort, I put Jimmy Phillips out of my head, trusting he was in better hands than mine, and went up to my room.

Rory was curled under the blankets, his hair spread over his pillow and mine, his breathing low and even. Black lashes rested on pale cheeks. He was the picture of peace. Undressing to my boxers, I climbed in behind him, scooped his hair off my pillow, and spooned against his back. He wiggled deeper into my embrace, snuggling under my arm.

"Gabe?"

"Go back to sleep, love."

"Mmm. Love."

"Yeah." I tightened my arm around his middle. "Love."

Chapter Eight

Rory

I woke with the light. I always had, coming into the world as the sun rose. Not that I was always eager to jump out of bed and start the day, but I never lingered, alone or not. It always seemed like a lonely place. But today I awoke with the weight of Gabe sprawled across me. His arm draped over my chest, and his leg pinned both of mine, like I belonged to him and even in his sleep he was going to keep what was his.

It was a comfortable place to be, and I would have been content to stay there, but my bladder had other ideas. Not wanting to wake him, I wiggled and contorted until I was free and slipped off to the bathroom. He was still asleep when I came back. I hesitated, unsure how to spend the free time. Normally, I would pull out my sketch book and get to work over a cup of coffee. Lately, my inspiration had pretty much dried up, and here I had nothing to work with. For the first time in weeks, I wanted a pencil and paper. I had something worth drawing.

I sat on the edge of the bed and watched Gabe sleep. He looked so much less stressed than he had since I'd met him. I wished there was some way I could preserve that relaxed feeling for him. If I couldn't do it with carbon and ink, maybe I could do it the only other way I knew how. I'd serve him breakfast and whatever else he wanted from me. Whatever he would accept. Anything he asked of me. He had enough to stress over. I wouldn't be one more thing to worry about. I'd show him he could trust me to do as he said.

"A good breakfast. Steak and eggs." And yogurt and fruit, which I'd fallen asleep without eating last night. I hoped Gabe would understand.

Half an hour later I was balancing a tray of food and coffee in one hand and pawing for the bedroom door handle with the other when the door opened and Gabe stood barring my way.

"I—" I swallowed, unable to read what he was thinking on his face. "I brought breakfast, Sir."

He nodded and took the tray from me, turning to carry it back into the room to the small sitting area across from the bed. He opened the drapes to a window that looked out onto a private back yard. The garden and view were well kept and soothing.

"Did you sleep well?" he asked as he drew his robe a little tighter around his waist and sat.

I nodded. "Yes, Sir." Nervous, because he wasn't giving me enough cues to figure out if I'd done something wrong, I stood there, just inside the door, pushing hair back behind my ear over and over as it kept falling back in my face.

"You need a hair elastic."

"Yes, Sir."

"Come here, Rory."

I went, trying to control my nerves, and stopped in front of him. It was extremely uncomfortable to have him looking up at me from his seat. I should have been at his feet, but he hadn't given me any indication what he wanted, and I couldn't read him. He didn't seem to notice, or if he did, he didn't care.

"I did some thinking last night, Rory."

"Yes, Sir." My voice tore on a whispery catch of nerves. My hands flew up to push hair off my face.

If he sent me away, where would I go? I couldn't go home. I frantically tried to think who I could call to help.

"I've decided you'll stay here with me at least until your house has been cleaned up. I'd prefer if you stay until I find Kane and put him behind bars where he belongs." He narrowed his eyes slightly and ran one hand down the tie of his robe over and over.

"Yes, Sir." Still a whisper, because I couldn't really breathe or process my good fortune.

"You want this?"

I nodded.

He waited, face still impassive, and I began to think maybe he was just offering because he had figured out I had no place else to go.

"I want this, Sir." I dropped to my knees in front of him so that I could get a little bit closer without towering over him. "I was hoping you would let me stay. I know you've been trying to get me to agree to that, then I thought you might find me some other place to stay where I'd be safe, but I want to stay with you."

He nodded, his gaze never leaving mine. I wish I knew what was going through his head.

"Come here." He took my hand and pulled me forward, tapped his thigh with his other hand. "Sit."

I couldn't help the smile that split my face and my mood wide open for him to see how happy that small invitation made me. I practically crawled into his lap.

"I have this dilemma now, Rory. You've given me a dilemma."

"I did?" I felt the smile slipping away.

He took the hand he was holding and drew it to his groin, pushing aside his robe so my palm pressed to his naked erection. "I have this wonderful smelling breakfast that will not be good to eat when it's cold, and I have this other matter that needs looking to."

His skin was hot and velvety under my palm. I thought I would melt with relief. "I can fix this."

"You created this situation. I should hope you can fix it."

"I need five minutes, please, to take care of breakfast, then I will take care of you."

"You have three."

He gave me a gentle shove and a light tap on the ass as I stood. I hurried breakfast back to the kitchen and into the oven to keep it warm, and was back at the foot of his chair in two and a half minutes.

His robe was wide open now, and he sat with his legs apart, his fingers slowly stroking his cock as he watched me kneel in front of him.

I didn't want to be nervous, but this was a familiar place. Nothing good had come of it for me yet. As kind as Gabe had been to me so far, Kane was still fresh, and I realised as much as I wanted Gabe, I couldn't escape Kane.

"You're terrified," Gabe whispered.

I didn't want to admit it. I kept my head down, too uncertain to admit my weakness. I should have known he wouldn't let me hide. His hand under my chin was so gentle. I lifted my head at the pressure of his fingers.

"It's okay to be scared. I can't imagine why you wouldn't be." He'd closed his robe and sat forward, this time pushing the hair off my face for me, caressing my lower lip with his thumb. "Sex only happens when you're ready for it to happen, and then only what you want."

I'd never once cried where Kane could see. Not through everything he did had I ever broken. Not in front of him. One bit of kindness from Gabe and I broke down like a baby. The tears welled and spilled before I even knew they were coming.

He slid onto the floor beside me, pulled me to him, sitting so both his legs came round me, then his arms, and he pressed his face into my hair. He didn't even shush me. He just held me.

I gulped breath after breath, trying to get myself under control. I'd had every intention of giving him the best blow job of his life while I was stashing our breakfast. He was everything I wanted. I couldn't let Kane ruin this chance. I wouldn't. Pulling myself together, I pushed off his chest and looked up at him. I knew my pale complexion would show off the puffy redness of my eyes and I'd be blotchy and flushed.

Then he kissed me.

My toes probably curled more than my hair, and my cock certainly didn't ignore his tongue in my mouth. I wasn't sure I could do anything about any of it right then, but it was good to be held, good to have someone who wanted to hold me, who could let me cry and then want me anyway. And who didn't expect me to do anything.

When Gabe finally let me go enough to look at me again, he had a tender smile, his hands still around my face, fingers in my hair. His eyes glazed over with need and concern, searching mine. I had no idea what for, but I felt for a minute like I owned him, and it was the most alive I could remember feeling in months.

"Ready for breakfast?" he asked, gruff and quiet, apparently satisfied with whatever he'd found in his search.

I nodded but held onto his wrists so he wouldn't get up.

"What is it?"

"I have to tell you some things."

"Okay."

"I think...I think you need to know because I want...I mean, I don't want you to be blindsided."

"By what?"

I took a deep breath. I had to say what was on my mind. I didn't want to be in a position where he was expecting something I couldn't give him. "It might not matter yet, but it will. At least, I hope it will." I encountered his hand when I tried to push at my hair, making me aware how often I made that gesture when I was nervous. My gaze fell from his face to rest on the thick fleece of his robe and the curling chest hairs revealed in the V. I was close enough to smell the warmth and sleep still clinging to him.

"I don't like fucking," I blurted. There was a pause. He didn't say anything. I couldn't look at him. "I'll do anything else you ask, I'm good at blow jobs and...other things, but I don't... It hurts. I don't like it."

I wound down and when I drew in another breath, he lifted my face.

"You're right. I do need to know that. It's good you told me."

"You're not mad? It's okay?"

"I'm not mad. Yes, it's fine. Is there anything else you don't like?"

"Being hit. Whipped. Nothing like that. It's horrible."

He nodded. I didn't think that would come as a big surprise to him, and he confirmed my assumption by kissing my forehead and assuring me he never had any intention of marking me in any way. "There are other ways to show you, and the world, that you belong to me, if you choose to accept them."

"Jewellery?" I teased, needing to lighten the mood some. "I like jewellery."

"Then you will positively sparkle. People will need sunglasses."

My laugh, admittedly, sounded more like a giggle, but it got me a tight squeeze, and I settled into his arms more securely.

"Is there anything else?"

"Restraints. I did like that, at first, but…"

"Okay. That's something we can work on."

We sat in silence for a little while. I thought about our breakfast desiccating in the oven but couldn't bring myself to actually move. "Gabe?"

"Mmm?"

"What changed?"

"Changed?"

"I thought you were going to tell me no. When I went to bed last night, I was sure you were going to send me off someplace else. I thought I made you uncomfortable. So what changed?"

"I forgot how simple some things are. Someone reminded me."

"A day and a half isn't very long." It seemed like a lifetime to me, but it was less than two days since this man had walked into my life, and I could feel forever in the way he held me now. It didn't make sense, but it was a gut-deep feeling. Like knowing I was gay, knowing I was submissive, knowing I was an artist. I knew I was Gabe's. I didn't question it because there was no question.

"Some things are very simple," he repeated.

Good enough for me. I squirmed around to face him and planted a kiss I hoped would wake up the erection he'd offered me earlier. It worked, but as I moved my kisses south, he leaned away, catching my chin and shaking his head. He took my hand, pressed it to his belly and nudged it downward.

"Hands only for now."

Logical, but painful—because I couldn't argue. I couldn't guarantee him I was safe. I didn't know for sure. I pulled my face out of his hand and rested my cheek against his chest.

He guided my hand over him, curling my fingers around his cock and his fingers around mine. His other hand stroked my hair, and his face once again burrowed into my curls. He seemed obsessed with my hair. It was okay. It meant I didn't have to look at him. I could absorb this latest humiliation without seeing his judgement.

"That's it," he whispered. "Just like that. You have wonderful hands."

So did he. Comforting. "I'm sorry."

"No need." He kissed me. I heard the soft snap of lips and felt the pressure. Goose bumps raised the little hairs over my scalp. "This is worth being careful. Taking our time." Another kiss followed by a gasp as I tightened my grip and picked up speed. "Doing it right. This is for keeps, Rory."

"Keeps." My hand on him faltered. "You—you want to keep me."

"As long as you want to stay."

For the moment, being an obedient submissive flew out the window. I pushed him onto his back and proceeded to kiss him over every available inch of skin I could find, smothering his face and throat and chest in affection while I humped him shamelessly.

He fumbled my jeans down enough to get his big hand on my cock and it took very little time, rubbing against his rough fingers and his own silky smooth cock, also trapped in his hand, to near that pinnacle.

"Almost..." I dropped my head and I found myself nuzzling into his neck.

He dropped his own cock and concentrated on me, slowing, dragging out the pleasure. It was heaven and torture the way he kept me on the edge without letting me drop over. His lips travelled over me, plucking up bits of flesh, tracing muscle and bone, lingering on each nipple until I was putty and begging.

Only I never wanted it to end.

Every touch was for me. His gaze never missed a single expression; he watched me and responded to every gasp. And he looked happy. He smiled at me when I met his gaze, and that pure expression of pleasure sent me over.

He kissed me as I came, and it scrambled my brain.

"Rory." A kiss on my neck. "Rory."

I blinked.

"Come on."

His hand was on mine, guiding it, and I felt his hard rod under my fingers.

God, I wanted to slide down and taste him. But I resisted. About that much, he was right. Until I knew for sure I was safe, I would abide by his rule. And forever after that if my stupidity had given me a life sentence. I wouldn't pass that on to him.

He caught my gaze, read every thought, because he smiled. "It's okay, love. One day at a time." He moved my hand over his dick. "One hand job at a time. Concentrate."

I did. Not a rope or chain in sight and he had me bound anyway, with his gaze. I couldn't free myself if I wanted to, which I didn't. I worked my way into his soul, sliding and twisting my hand over his cock until his lids drooped and he gasped, body tightening, warm cum spurting over my fist.

"Oh, Rory."

More kisses covered me. I lay back and took them. Eventually, he wound down. His weight crushed me comfortably against the shag rug.

"Breakfast will be ruined," I informed him.

"I'll take you out."

"Denny's?"

"Puh-lease." He backed up and held out a hand to help me up. "Get dressed. Something nice."

"I have one outfit."

"Oh. Right." He shrugged. "Jeans will do."

Gabe

Rory took himself and his clothes off to the bathroom and I let him go in alone, both to give him an opportunity to get his own bearings, and to give myself a chance to ease into this. I pushed myself back up into my chair, used a few tissues to clean up, and sat for a minute, staring at the sodden mass wondering how much of it was his. A whole new emotional quagmire surrounded the fact he hadn't argued whether or not he was safe. I could only appreciate his honesty and help him deal with whatever he found out. I didn't want to imagine a scenario under which he didn't know what risks he'd been forced to take. That line of thought only made me want to hurt someone and wasn't going to help him, or me.

Instead, I made an appointment at the clinic for both of us for that afternoon, though mine was just for moral support, and went to join him in the shower. I might have lingered over his half-hard cock and enticed another orgasm out of him, but his stomach growled loud enough to echo a bit, which made him blush pink. That particular shade of gorgeous wasn't conducive to me not wanting him, but I rallied my resolve.

"If you don't get out of this shower now, Rory, I fear you'll faint from hunger before I'm through with you."

"Am I that irresistible, then?" He batted his eyelashes at me, blushing prettily to go along with the wicked smile.

He wasn't, for one second, letting me forget the innocent exterior wasn't all he had.

I kissed him, hard, leaving no doubt in his mind just how irresistible I found him.

"Right, then," he breathed, the words barely heard over another rumble of his stomach while he leaned bonelessly against me and looked up.

No more eyelash batting. No sultry smiles. Just that wide open expanse of Rory looking out of the endless depths of his eyes, full of all he was. Yesterday, I'd seen him waiting for someone to come along and fill him. Today, he was there, sure of himself, offering what he had, waiting, not to be filled, but to fill me.

"Breakfast, Sir?"

I took a moment to pull in a deep breath, just to look at him, take my fill. "Yeah." He knew he had me. I could see it in his eyes, and he was proud of himself.

He stepped out of the shower all grace and calm and proceeded to dry himself off, completely unselfconscious of his body. It gave me a chance to assess his condition. The marks were more faded. The small, open sores had closed nicely. His hip and shoulder bones were too prominent, and I could see his ribs. It was disconcerting to think he'd done that to himself to please a monster like Kane.

As though he felt my eyes on him, his movement slowed, stopped, and he turned to look at me. His towel dropped to the floor, and he stood, arms at his sides.

I turned off the shower, opened the door, and picked up a towel to dry my own face.

"His marks will fade soon, Sir."

"They will. Do they hurt?"

"Not anymore. I can't put the cream on them that Gina gave me, though."

"Get it."

"Yes, Sir."

He sat quietly while I spread the stuff over his welts. The feel of his ribs, the knobs of his spine through his skin, was difficult to stomach, not because he disgusted me, but because I understood the mind set he'd been reduced to, that he thought he had to do such a thing. Because I cared about him that much already and I knew, for Kane to get that deep into his head, he'd had to have done some terrible things to Rory. Things that were not going to be undone in just one weekend. Things it might take a lifetime to undo. I'd never hated before. It was unpleasant in the extreme.

"They'll heal faster with the cream." He couldn't even see me, yet he spoke as though he knew I needed comforting. "I'll heal now." He turned to face me as I was capping the cream. "I remember who I am, Gabe. I forgot for a while, couldn't find myself. But more and more, I remember. It's going to be okay. Even when it seems like I'm lost, I know I'll always find my way back to you."

"It's only been two days."

"Don't ask me to explain it. I just know it's right."

He was an amazing man. I couldn't believe my luck, but I wasn't about to question it. Right in that moment, with him looking up at me with so much honesty, I could believe anything. Even that Kane couldn't touch us.

I took him to Peter's. I'd called while Rory was off dressing and made sure Peter would be there. It would give Rory a chance to speak to Peter and Adam one at a time. Less intimidating. I still felt a twinge of guilt at his reaction the day before. The two of them together could be overwhelming. I hadn't thought about that when I needed them. It had been a while since I had to think of anyone but myself. It would take some adjustment, but there was nothing I was more willing to do than rearrange my life to accommodate Rory.

We sat at the counter rather than one of the booths, and I *almost* didn't puff up with pride when we walked in and he stayed by my side, stood beside me until I motioned for him to sit. He did, smiling contentedly.

Peter came out then, and I knew from the snap in his eyes he'd seen us enter and had been watching.

"Hey." I held out a hand and we shook. "Peter, this is Rory. Rory, Peter."

"Rory." Peter nodded.

Rory greeted him, dropped his gaze, and laid his hands flat on the counter. "I'm sorry for my behaviour yesterday, Sir. It was an insult for me to assume anything about you and your companion. I hope you can forgive me."

"Under the circumstances, Rory, I don't think there is anything to forgive. We all should have been more careful and more sensitive."

"Does everyone know?" he asked quietly, sounding horrified by the idea.

Peter leaned closer so their conversation was private. "Look at me, please, Rory."

I did my best not to bristle at the tone of command. He was only taking control of the situation, being sure he had Rory's attention because what he had to say was important. I managed to keep my mouth shut.

Rory lifted his head, automatically glancing at me, and I nodded reassurance, somewhat mollified by his deference. He turned his attention back to Peter.

"Gabe doesn't choose to share his confidence with just anyone. If he does tell someone something, it's because he trusts us. Do you believe even for a moment he would ever betray you or your trust?"

"No, Sir." No hesitation, no flinching. He had that much faith in me already.

"You have friends here, Rory."

Rory nodded.

It pained me to see doubt in his eyes. Like he wasn't used to the idea of having friends. I reached over and took his hand. "Coffee, love?"

"Yes, please."

All his confidence seemed to have evaporated. His fingers were tight around my hand. Like this morning when a bit of consideration had undone him, Peter's kind words seemed to have shaken him.

As Peter moved off, I squeezed his fingers. "All right?"

He nodded and swivelled towards me a bit, though he kept his face turned down. "I was so rude." His long, graceful fingers pushed a bit of hair behind his ear, though it didn't go very far towards moving the copious locks out of his face. "He wasn't even a bit angry, and neither were you. I just…I can't believe how wrong I had everything."

"Kane made sure you had no way of understanding how it works. That is not your fault."

The coffee arrived. Rory gave Peter a shy smile of thanks, and we took the mugs to a more private booth. His unsettled demeanour calmed considerably as he ate, and this time, though he didn't nearly finish everything Peter had piled onto his plate, I was satisfied that he'd had a decent meal. He practically glowed with happiness by the time we finished.

"I knew I was not going to be able to stand it," Peter muttered as he picked up our finished plates and refilled our mugs.

"Shut it," I muttered, hiding my own deep-seated content behind my mug.

"Beyond sickening."

"Because you and Adam aren't saccharine at all."

He grinned. "How the mighty have fallen. Rory, you should be proud."

"I am."

I raised one eyebrow at that bit of cheek. He just grinned back. In that moment, I couldn't think of a time I had ever enjoyed more than seeing him happy and confident.

Peter groaned and wandered off.

"What will we do now, Sir?"

"Well, you need more than one outfit, for starters."

"You don't strike me as the shopping type."

Observant of him. "And you are?" I loved the way he had absolutely no control over the way his pale skin coloured with every emotion. "Then it is a good thing my credit is at your disposal."

"I don't need you to buy me things. I have money."

I tipped my head. "Did I say you needed it?"

"No, Sir."

"And where is your wallet? Your credit cards? Your bank card?"

"Okay. I get it."

"Then indulge me."

"Let you keep me?" He was keeping his eyes on his coffee, very carefully not looking at me.

"I already told you I would. This is not about you being a kept man, Rory. It's about me doing something useful and you letting me."

For a few silent minutes, I watched him fiddle with the handle of his mug. There was some other question he was struggling to ask. Or maybe trying not to ask. I reached over and laid my fingers gently over his nervous twitch. His other hand, predictably, moved to push the hair away from his face.

"Ask," I said.

"Ask what?"

"Whatever it is you're trying not to."

His eyes remained fixed on his drink, his lips sealed.

"Once again, I remind you, I can't help you if you hold back."

"Am I not allowed any privacy?"

"Whatever is on your mind is affecting your ability to even look at me, to accept my offer. It's obviously important enough to frighten you."

"Fine." He set his jaw, pulled his hand free, and looked at me. "What will it cost me?"

"Cost you?"

Still, his gaze skidded away from mine.

I drew in a calming breath. "Well, let me see. I take you shopping, which means I get to watch you model whatever I pick for you to try on, imagine what it will be like to get you out of those same clothes, and hopefully, I get to see you smile once or twice. And all it costs *me* is a few pennies. The way I figure it, I'm already getting the better end of this bargain."

He nodded slowly, his gaze finally stopping. He looked into my eyes, and I was impressed by his control and the determination I saw there.

"Okay. But I do have my own money."

"Money you are going to need to replace a lot more than a few pairs of jeans and tees. And anyway, I have more. In fact, I have more money than I can ever reasonably spend on myself, so let me do this and no more arguments." I smiled gently. "I am the boss of you, Rory, and it's my prerogative to spoil you rotten if I so choose."

He smiled at last, and I let out a little huff of relief.

"Still," he said, once again shoving his hair aside, "I should be allowed to thank you in some way."

"I will let you decide how you want to do that." I sat back and picked up my coffee. "In the meantime, where would you like to go first?"

"I'm not even sure. I don't suppose you do malls?"

I laughed but nodded. "I could. For you. But we have to be back here by three."

"What happens at three?"

I hated to spoil his hard-won relaxed mood, but it wasn't fair I not tell him about the clinic.

He just nodded in response. "Okay. I can do a lot of damage to your bank balance in that amount of time." When he looked at me, he surprised me yet again with his strength. "Thank you for taking care of that. The sooner we know, the better, right?"

"You are absolutely right. That was my thinking as well. And the nurse can have a quick look at your back, although I think it's healing nicely. Nothing to worry about, really."

"You really do take good care of me," he said, his voice low and far too full of what sounded like awe.

"You deserve it."

"Because I've been through so much —"

I could hear the bitterness rising and cut him off. "Because you are you, and I want to see you smile. It's purely selfish."

"Liar."

But he smiled and let go of some tension, and even though I knew he would never say it, I suspect a part of him wanted to just be free of responsibility and decision-making. For one day, I could give him that. It wasn't a solution to his problems, but it would let him decompress enough to think more clearly. Before we made any permanent decisions about anything, he needed to be thinking clearly. I was not about to examine the clutching worry that gripped me when I acknowledged once he was thinking like himself again, he may not want me. This wasn't about me.

Chapter Nine

Rory

Gabe hated every minute of the mall. I could see it in the way he scowled when he thought I wasn't looking, the way his head swivelled in every direction, as though he thought someone was going to jump out of the penny fountain or the escalator was going to suck him in, pant legs first. It was touching that he endured it for me, and in a way, a little bit funny. I didn't spare time to contemplate his apparent paranoia might be justified. I knew too little about Kane and his habits. There was no way to be completely confident he wouldn't show up anywhere, any time.

After the first two shops, an H&M and The Bay, I started to suspect he was not just having a horrible time, but that he had cottoned on to my attempt to get a decent number of items at a reasonable price. I didn't really want to break his bank. I wanted to pay him back eventually, so I had to at least try to stay within my own means.

"No." He shook his head at the outfit I had on, the fourth one I'd modelled and the fourth one he'd said no to.

"Worried I look too sexy?" I asked, examining my woefully flat bottom in the mirror.

"Are you?" He lifted his eyebrows, that look I'd figured out meant I wasn't to shit him on my answer.

"I look skinny and underfed."

"Take it off. We'll find something. Doesn't anyone in this frightful place sell Hugo Boss?"

"Frightful?" I snickered. "Darling, your gay is showing."

"Well. I'm gay enough to want my lover to look presentable when I take him out to dinner. Get changed."

"Yes, Sir." I took the time to peck his cheek, though, and whisper my thanks in his ear, even though we hadn't purchased anything yet beyond a couple of hair clips with just a tiny bit of bling to keep them from disappearing entirely into my mass of curls.

It had been refreshing to see the way he smiled at me when he caught me eyeing them in the aisle kiosk. I didn't normally indulge in my slightly girlier tendencies where anyone could see. Another of my quirks Kane had mercilessly tried to beat out of me. Gabe just brought out his wallet and handed his card to the clerk, then watched quietly while I arranged my hair.

When I'd presented the final effect, full of nerves almost to the point of shaking, he just nodded and smiled, leaning close for a soft kiss on my cheek.

"It looks okay?"

"Who knew watching you do your hair would be such a massive turn-on," he assured me.

The clerk might have blushed deeper than I did as we both glanced at Gabe's crotch. But I made a mental note. So many fascinating sides to my Gabriel.

We were leaving the mall when my attention caught on the last shop before the exit. It was the massive art supply store where I usually got my markers and paper. They had decent products and decent prices. Gabe saw me eyeing the place and slowed his hasty dash for escape.

"I don't even know if any of my own stuff is still useable," I admitted.

"You can probably get back into your place tomorrow to find out."

I nodded.

"Do you want to go in?"

I nodded again.

He indulged me, and I led him straight to the sketch books where I picked out two sizes. He followed me around until I had pencils, markers, all manner of little odds and ends. He asked what each one was for as though he actually cared what the answer was. It was fun to talk about something I knew so well, something that mattered to me. And when I looked into Gabe's face, it was alight with happiness — a new and fascinating expression on his usually very reserved face.

"What?" He smiled down on me as we wandered to the cash, his hand light on the small of my back.

"You just look so happy."

"So do you. Do you have everything you need?"

I looked over my stash one more time. "I think so. It's been so long since I felt like drawing anything at all. My publisher is probably freaking out. I'm going to have to call her soon."

"Tomorrow."

"Yes, Sir."

I smiled at him, and we waited patiently as the cashier tallied up. The total made my eyes bug a bit, though I knew my profession wasn't a cheap one to outfit, especially from scratch. Gabe just footed the bill and took a few of the parcels, and we left the shop.

Out in the wide hallway, the crowds had multiplied exponentially. Gabe frowned, pulled me a little closer with just a look, and we made our way towards the exit.

I heard his voice first. That smooth, cold voice that had sentenced me to so much pain. It cut through the noise of the shoppers like ice. It froze my heart, my feet. I suddenly couldn't breathe, and Gabe took another step, two. I lost track of him in the sea of people. I could hear Kane talking, the measured clomp of his boots, felt a hand on my back.

"Rory."

My throat closed. I couldn't call out. My carefully wrapped packages fell, scattered at my feet. All I knew was that hand, the hot breath on my cheek. I closed my eyes against the dizzying, immobilising fear.

"I know where he's keeping you." A hand twisted in my hair, grinding my new clip into my scalp and pulling my head back. "Gabriel Stark is not going to win this one. You tell him I said so."

Then he was gone. I whirled, saw the swish of his coat, a boot, and the crowd swallowed him up.

"Rory. What happened?" Gabe was there.

He touched my hair and I pulled away.

"Don't!"

"Hey." He peered at me, concerned.

"He—he was here." My voice shook. My entire body shook. "He…" I lifted a hand to my head but dropped it again without touching. I could still feel the pain where the clip had dug in. Another mark. Kane's filthy fingers on Gabe's first gift to me.

"Kane?" Gabe was digging his phone out of his pocket, dialling a number, looking frantically around us. "Come on."

"My parcels!" I couldn't leave them behind. I yanked free of Gabe's hold and dashed back for them.

We gathered them and hurried out, not stopping until we were in the car. Gabe talked to someone named Adam, listened and nodded. "We'll be right there."

He started the car, and I sat, parcels clutched to me like they were armour enough to hold off the memory of that horrible encounter and every other time Kane had touched me.

"Where are we going?"

"Police station. My friend Adam—he was at the house yesterday, too—he'll ask you some questions, okay?"

"Yes, Sir." Anything he said. I clung to that, fell into the easy obedience, confident he'd do what was necessary. "Then we can go home? I want to get him off me."

"Off you? Did he touch you?"

I nodded.

"Where?"

"My hair. He…" I made a vague motion towards my head, and this time he was the one who told me not to touch.

"If there's any chance he left something behind…"

"My clip. He had it in his grip, too." My fingers hovered over the pretty bauble. "I'll have to give it to them."

"Probably."

That, more than the words Kane had said, more than the threat I didn't even understand, made me angry. It was mine, and it seemed everything I owned, however briefly, he was determined to taint and ruin. "I hate him."

Gabe glanced over at me but didn't say a word. I could see my feelings reflected in his eyes, though he didn't say it. "I'm so sorry, love."

"For what?"

"Two seconds. Two steps." His voice broke, and I looked again. It wasn't hate in his eyes. It was fear. For me. "It could have been so much—"

"It wasn't worse." I wouldn't even let him contemplate the thought of what Kane could have done to me in those two seconds. If he'd intended to hurt me, I suddenly felt certain he would not have done so unless he was sure Gabe was there to witness it. No. It was a warning that he *could*. It wasn't a warning for me. It wasn't an attempt to hurt me, but to hurt my Gabriel. "It isn't about me," I muttered.

"What?"

I half turned in my seat. "It isn't about me. It never was. It's you."

"What are you talking about?"

"He said you wouldn't win this one."

"Win what one? Rory, you aren't making any sense."

I thought back, closing my eyes to block out his repeated, worried glances and remember. "He said, 'I know where he's keeping you. Gabriel Stark is not going to win this one. Tell him I said so.'" I opened my eyes to find Gabe staring at me.

He'd pulled over to the kerb and we sat, frozen.

"Those were his exact words. That's what he said to me. This is about you. It's all been about you. Everything…"

His eyes went wide, he paled. Complete horror took over his expression. My gut churned as I saw the realisation invade his thoughts. Everything Kane had put me through had led to Gabe. He'd orchestrated everything right up to Gabe taking me in, every single step. Because somehow, he knew what everyone involved would do. Which meant he was one of them, and not one of them knew who he was.

"No." My own voice didn't sound like mine. "No. He can't have this too." I grabbed up Gabe's hand from the steering wheel and brought it to my lips. "This is us. Ours. He didn't do this. We did. Don't let him take it, Gabe, please. I couldn't stand it if he took this, too. Please."

Gabe wrenched his hand free, turned back to the wheel, and hit the gas. The next few minutes were a whirlwind of frightful driving culminating in Gabe squealing rubber into the police parking lot. He jumped out of the car, came round and hauled my door open. I sat in frozen disbelief as everything fell apart around me.

But he didn't pull me out, drag me into the building as I expected. He dropped into a crouch beside me. "Rory. Rory, love, look at me."

His voice was so gentle. Calm. It penetrated, and I managed to do as he asked.

"You're right. He can't have this. He isn't going to win anything, least of all you. Trust me, love. We have to go inside. Adam is waiting."

I nodded and took his hand. He led me inside, past hundreds of people I didn't see. I only followed along in his wake, keeping my eyes on his back and my fingers curled tight around his hand. I was not letting him out of my sight again.

We were taken to a small office where we waited less than five minutes before another man joined us. He was huge. His dress slacks and shirt and tie, all in shades of taupe and brown, looked flimsy and insubstantial on his enormous frame. I remembered the glimpse of his furry barrel chest and massive thighs encased in leather.

He nodded amicably and settled on the desk, hands clasped in front of him. He wore a heavy gold ring on his left ring finger, and a tattoo on his inner wrist depicted a beautifully inked monogram. "So. You're Rory Sanders."

I nodded. "Yes, Sir."

A quick glance at Gabe told me I was on my own for a minute. He stood with his back to us, looking out the office window at the larger space and people beyond. I could tell he needed a moment to process.

I stood and held out my hand to the police officer. "You were at our—Gabe's—house yesterday."

He nodded. "Adam Keller."

His grip was warm, firm, his hand dwarfing mine to child-size, but without one ounce of the pressure he was most certainly capable of.

"When you were visiting, I behaved rather badly," I told him, as though it were remotely possible he didn't know that. "I'm very sorry for making such a grievous assumption. It was rude."

"We should have been more sensitive. Under the circumstances, it's not at all surprising you reacted the way you did. I'm very sorry for frightening you."

I just stared at him, unable to even let go of his hand. How was it possible to have stumbled across so many people who not only seemed able to accept without blinking an eye everything I was and was not, but even seemed able to understand? I'd never made friends easily and I'd lost those I'd had over a lifestyle choice that had done me nothing but harm to this point. It was incredible to find the entire world was not against the idea that love might take a different form.

Behind me, Gabe cleared his throat softly. "Rory."

"Uh…" I snatched my hand back.

Adam just smiled. "Down, boy." He grinned at Gabe, but it only lasted a second before he was back perched on his desk, arms crossed over his chest. "So. Gabe said you saw Kane?"

"Um, well, no. I mean. He came up behind me. I didn't see. He took my hair…"

Gabe's hand circled my wrist, and I realised I'd lifted my hand to where Kane had gripped me. "Don't touch, love. Adam, you'll want to collect that clip."

Adam nodded, poked his head out the door, and a few minutes later we were joined by a woman with a plethora of tools. She had me sit on the couch, and for the next half hour, I was the centre of her careful attention as she donned latex gloves and more patience than I could imagine. She combed out every strand of my hair, catching anything that fell on slips of paper, and retrieved the clip in a tiny baggie. She took it all away with her, and Gabe made me sit a few more minutes as he cleaned the cut on my scalp with hydrogen peroxide and a cotton swab.

I stifled the ache when he donned gloves to do it, but I knew we had already committed to being very careful. All the while, Adam asked question after question, not just about the encounter in the mall, but about my house and what had happened in the club, as well. The technician gathering her samples hadn't batted an eyelash at his explicit questions or my halting answers. Gabe just held my hand and said nothing.

"There isn't a lot else we can do right now, Gabe," Adam said, when he had asked all the questions he could think of and I'd given all the answers I cared to.

It had been exhausting in a way nothing else I'd ever done had been. Gabe just slid an arm around me when I leaned on him, and rubbed a hand up and down my arm.

When he spoke, his voice remained as quiet and matter of fact as he'd been since we'd entered the station. "He's in danger, Adam. You see that."

"Sounds to me like you both are."

I felt a slight tightening of tension run through Gabe, and he said, "I don't know who he is, Adam, so don't ask."

Adam's gaze was steady as he studied my lover, waiting.

"I don't know." For the first time since entering Adam's office, Gabe sounded put out, almost angry with his friend.

Still, Adam's expression didn't change. "When's the last time you heard from Darnel?"

"Nichols?" Gabe moved away from me slightly. "No."

"Gabe, it's worth considering."

"You didn't see him at the funeral, Adam. He was devastated. And I know he has issues but this?" Gabe shook his head in denial, the look in his eyes contradicting the motion. Adam had apparently presented him with a scenario he didn't want to believe.

"Who is he?"

Adam sighed. "An old acquaintance."

"I knew his ex," Gabe said, his voice a bland monotone. "Long time ago. It isn't him."

I glanced at Adam and he was still studying Gabe with that shrewd detective glare.

Gabe bristled and pulled me back, close against his side. "You can put the cop glare away, Adam."

The timbre of command rippled through Gabe's voice and made me shiver. I stiffened, hearing him direct it another man.

Adam's lips tightened slightly and he frowned. "Back off, Gabby. I'm doing my job." He seemed uncomfortable and the fingers of his right hand caressed the tattoo on his left wrist. He suddenly didn't seem to know where to look.

I glared at Adam, snuggling closer to Gabe. I might as well have shouted, *Mine!*

Adam gave me a little nod and moved around behind his desk. "Prickly little thing."

I made a face. "I'm tired. Some asshole has been playing games with my life for mysterious reasons all his own, I'm late for my AIDS test, and you have my jewellery. You're lucky 'prickly' is all I am."

"I will buy you more jewellery, Rory," Gabe assured me. "And the clinic can wait."

"No. It can't." I turned back to Adam. "The condom from my house."

"What about it?" He leant forward, setting his elbows on top of the paperwork spread across the surface.

"Did you test it?"

"A DNA test is being done. But you have to understand, unless Kane has committed some sort of felony, and been caught, there's very little chance we have his DNA on file. With today's attack, maybe, if he left anything on that hair clip, and we can match the samples… Technically, it still doesn't put him in your house, though. It's possible someone else got hold of that condom—"

"I mean, did you test it for HIV?"

He blinked at me. "It never occurred to us."

"Well you should, although I'm pretty sure I already know what you'll find. It probably isn't his and it'll be positive." I rose and turned to pull Gabe up after me. "Let's go."

"Wait." Adam rose from behind his desk and rounded it, moving on instinct, maybe, but putting his bulk between us and the door. "Explain."

I sighed and sat back down. This was going to come out eventually, anyway. I told them about Kane's most severe punishment, when he blindfolded, shackled and shared me. The threats he'd whisper in my ear, that I had no idea what they might be infecting me with, had been the worst. And in truth, I didn't know. I hadn't been able to protect myself, and the condom he'd left in my house would be just another reminder, another threat that he controlled me, even from afar. His own private, sick joke. It was a measure of how deeply he had controlled me that I hadn't gone and gotten myself tested before now. Maybe I'd just resigned myself to the consequences of my own idiocy.

I didn't flinch from looking them in the eye. What I felt inside didn't matter. Kane wanted to take everything. If he'd planned on giving Gabe a broken husk of a man, someone he couldn't save, he had another think coming. Whatever my test results, every second of my life from here forward was going to be about Gabe and his happiness. Kane's first mistake had been assuming I was as fragile on the inside as I appeared on the outside. Maybe I was. But Gabe showed me I didn't have to stay that way. His second was threatening Gabe.

Gabe

The clinic visit was quick. Rory refused to put it off even a day, and it was a small enough concession to give him back that much of the control he clearly needed. It was gratifying to know he wasn't about to roll over and take any more. At home, he unpacked the bags from the art store and laid them all out on the kitchen table. The process seemed to restore his good spirits, for which I was grateful, because I was at a loss how to do that. I was murderously angry myself and feared it would show the minute he looked into my eyes. Watching him gradually calm and relax as he lovingly turned out the tools of his trade had a remarkably similar effect on me.

"Would it be all right if I set up a workspace in the spare room?" he asked then tore at the last blister pack with his teeth. "The light is good. I can move the bed to the corner."

I handed him a pair of scissors — again — as he spat out a hunk of cardboard. "We'll move the bed to the basement for storage. Do you need a desk?"

He gazed steadily at me. "If we dismantle the bed, that only leaves one bed in the house."

"Do we need more than one?" I deliberately looked him up and down. "You're not very big. I barely noticed the lump —"

He smacked me. "I use a draft table."

"Those are a lot more expensive than desks, I bet."

"Very much, yes. I'll have to replace my computer, too."

"I have an old laptop."

"I need a Mac. Better graphics."

"And higher price tag."

"Yes." He settled against the table across from where I was sitting and began ticking things off on his fingers. "Then I only picked up a few things today. I'll need a full set of markers, a larger sketch book, a back light table, a portfolio, a set of French curves, Exacto knives, rulers, a cutting pad, and a scanner."

"You done?"

"I think so. That'll get me started, anyway."

"Good, because I have something for you. Not on your rather extensive list, but I picked it up while you were with the nurse. I know it's not as pretty as the first one. I had to settle for the small selection at the jeweller's next door to the clinic, and I didn't have a lot of time to choose." I handed him a small package, gift wrapped, and prayed he'd like it.

His hands shook a bit as he opened it. This clip was smaller than the one he'd had to give up to Adam. It was black and rimmed on one edge with a few tiny diamonds. Nothing spectacular, but it had made him so happy the first time.

I held my breath.

He looked from me to the gift and back again.

"If you don't like it, we can return it. You can pick —"

"You bought me diamonds?"

"Only very tiny ones."

"Nobody ever bought me diamonds before." He was staring at the thing like he'd never seen anything like it.

"I know it's not really big enough to hold much of that mop back —"

"Shut up." He straddled my lap and wrapped his arms around my neck. "I love it, Gabe."

"Good. Put it in."

He examined it again, then me. "Does it really turn you on?"

"I'm as shocked as you, believe me."

"Because I'm not wearing a dress or anything."

"No." I placed my hands on his ass and looked up at him. "Of course not. You're all man. It isn't that it's feminine. It's…how you look. Your expression. Put it in."

His smile was gentle, and his kiss pure pleasure and want, leaving me panting and hard when he pulled away. I watched him sweep his hair back, slip the clip in place and fasten it. Maybe it was about the action itself, a little bit. Because he was so fantastically sexy and confident inside that skin of the man who wanted a pretty hair clip. I wondered idly if watching him draw would make me cream my pants.

"What are you thinking?"

"That you are an incredibly sexy man."

"I've felt skinny and scared for a very long time," he admitted. "Today was the first time in my life I have ever actually been in public with my hair back. I thought it would feel weird."

"And did it?" I gazed up at him, pulled him a little closer, and settled both hands on his ass to hold him in place.

"No." He was practically whispering, but there was a deep satisfaction behind his words. "It felt like I was finally allowed to be me. It just felt good. Right." His gaze drifted, further away, though his hands remained around my neck and he didn't seem upset. Just thoughtful.

"I've never been ashamed of being gay, you know," he said at last. "I had friends who didn't care. But when I started going to clubs with Kane, when my friends realised what kind of clubs they were…" He shook his head sadly. "It was like I was fifteen again. Back home, where I could be gay as long as no one knew and I didn't do anything that would embarrass my family. Seems like all my life I've been trying to make other people happy, and not one of them cared if I was happy."

He settled a little, making himself comfortable. "When I was about fourteen, just starting high school, I had this stash of hair stuff my sister had given me. I've always had long hair, and it gets in the way when I'm drawing. So she gave me some of her stuff to help keep it out of my face. I used to bring them to school, so I could use them in art class. One day, I had this pink thing. A cat, I think. It was cute. But I forgot to take it out. You can imagine what that was like in a high school in small town shitsville. I went home with a black eye and a fat lip. When my father heard what had happened, you know what he did?"

"I hope he kicked some punk ass into the next county."

"I hoped he would too."

"But?"

"He turned my room upside down, sacked everything, until he found the hair stuff. Threw it all in the trash compactor, marched me downtown, and stood over me while some poor woman shaved my head. I thought she was going to cry."

"I'm sorry, Rory."

"He locked me in my room until it was cleaned up and made me pay to get the trash compactor fixed, too. Bastard. I spent the next two years working a part time job, talking to my art teacher. He taught me how to approach agents and publishers, helped me get some contracts. I saved every penny until I was sixteen, moved out, and spent the next two years finishing high school and drawing manga, living in a shit-box apartment on ramen and Dr Pepper and paying my rent through my ass.

"But I graduated, and I sold a series concept. It paid an advance. I sold another. I got a house, I worked, I drew. I did it, Gabe. I did it by myself. I've never let anyone tell me I couldn't do it, that I wasn't capable of supporting myself. I never doubted myself. Not in that."

He fell silent. It wasn't what he'd told me that darkened his face and kept him staring off into space. It was what he stopped short of saying.

"It's strange to think," he said softly, "that all the time I've been trying to satisfy everyone, and now, here with you, it means more to me to make you happy and proud of me than it ever has with anyone, and yet, for once, it doesn't feel like I'm compromising anything." His gaze snapped back to me, and he smiled brightly. "Not even my silly little hair clips."

"Definitely not those." The image that popped into my head, of him standing in my kitchen in nothing but that little diamond clip sweeping his hair away from his face, had me hard and aching in seconds. I wanted him. There were so many issues to deal with. I wanted to shower him with love and comfort and keep him safe, and he wanted to get his own feet back under him and stand on his own. I couldn't help but wonder if he would still want me as much once he was feeling like himself again.

"You know what I want right now?" he asked, drawing me back to the current situation involving him seated solidly there in my lap.

"Tell me."

"I'm allowed to do that?"

"Always. In fact, it is a firm requirement." I smiled and reached up to touch his hair. It wasn't in his face anymore, but I loved the way the silky smooth curls entangled my fingers and whispered against my skin. "I might veto it, if I think it's not good for you. You have to trust me on that. I'll always listen and do my best to make sure you have what you need, but I must always know what you want."

"You wouldn't veto a bubble bath, would you?"

"Absolutely not."

"Would you join me?"

"Just try and keep me out."

His eyes got serious. "If I wanted to keep you out..."

"Love, you know the answer to that. Nothing unless you want it." I trailed my fingers through his hair and cupped the nape of his neck. Like always, he shivered and slipped into a lip-parted haze, his gaze soft. "That, right there," I whispered, "is the most precious thing anyone has ever given me, Rory. The expression on your face, the look in your eye that says you trust me not to take too much. Anyone who doesn't understand the strength that takes..." I shook my head. "Unbelievable he thought he could break that."

"You don't think I'm weak and broken?"

I shook my head. "No."

"Damaged."

"Hurt, Rory. Impossible not to be hurt."

"Gabe, if those tests come back positive—"

"Hush, now. We agreed. No speculation. We get results tomorrow and deal with the answer when it comes."

"I'm scared."

"I know." I stood, but rather than let his feet drop to the floor, he wrapped his legs around my hips. I adjusted to take his weight. "I am too. It's scary. I want to keep you a very long time, and either way, I intend to. "

"A life sentence, though, Gabe."

"That's right." I headed towards the stairs. "A life sentence by my side, serving me, drawing your cartoons and growing your hair to your waist so I can deck it out in every pretty thing I can get my hands on."

His answer was to bury his face against my neck and wrap his arms around me. Not a declaration of undying love, but not a refusal of my offer, either. It would have to do.

He was settled under the bubbles, once again nestled between my legs when he finally spoke. "It's manga."

"Sorry?"

"Manga. Not cartoons, or comics. Manga."

I nodded. "Yaoi manga. I know. I looked it up."

"You did?"

"Of course I did."

"When?"

"The night you got here. I wanted to know what I was dealing with. I found your website and Twitter, your Facebook." I watched him in the mirror as he flushed.

"You know everything about me…"

"Hardly. You present a very professional face online, Rory. Your fans love you, which is hardly surprising, and you do lovely work. I'm not in the least surprised you can support yourself with your talent. But that is hardly all there is to know about you."

"No," he agreed quietly. "If I looked you up online, I wouldn't find anything, would I?"

"I hope not. In my line of work, it isn't wise to be overly accessible."

"And which line would that be? The private eye or the professional Dom?"

"Both."

He nodded. "What happens when this Rolly person calls you with a man he wants you to train?"

"Are you expressing some desire I turn the offer down?"

"Yes." His voice was flat, firm.

He didn't look at me, but he was stiff in my arms. Rather than be annoyed he thought he could have an opinion on the matter, I felt pride in him that he would speak up for what he wanted. It gave me hope he was strong enough to overcome what Kane had done to him.

"Am I to understand, then, that you want me to effectively retire from a very lucrative job?"

"I want you not to be having sex with anyone else."

Under the rigid set of his shoulders, I felt the tremor, maybe fear I would refuse his request or punish him for making it.

"Fair enough. I'll call Rolly in the morning."

"You will?" Water splashed over the edges of the tub as he sat up. "You'll stop? Just because I asked?" He slipped and barely caught himself from going under as he spun. Suds and water sloshed everywhere. "You'd do that for me?"

I'd sent Jimmy away for him. I'd do a whole lot more, including giving up a pastime that had all but lost its sparkle already anyway. "I'll do whatever it takes to help you heal."

His brow furrowed. "Including figuring out why Kane did this? Who he is? What he was trying to prove?" He swallowed hard, but his chest heaved, and he breathed through parted lips. "It was never about me at all. All of that—"

"Was because of me. Because he knew exactly what he had to do to get me to take notice. I'm sorry it was at your expense. I will find out who he is and what he wants, Rory. I promise."

"It seems so strange."

"What does?"

"To know he never cared anything about me. That I was just another tool to him. Not human at all." There was dark purpose in his gaze when he met my eye. "I never would have been able to avoid any of it, no matter what I did. It was all about figuring out what he had to do to make me hurt the most, to get me to break. He wanted me completely his pathetic creature. He wanted to show you a shell of a human being, someone you couldn't fix. Why does he hate you so much?"

"I wish I knew."

"I have to…" For a minute, Rory hung there, indecision keeping him poised between kneeling between my legs and standing. He chose to stand. "I don't know what to do." He stood there uncertainly, the delayed reaction of knowing how horribly Kane had used him making him shake and curl in on himself. "Tell me what to do."

I stepped out of the tub and put a hand on his shoulder. "Sit. Get warm and just relax. I'll make you something to eat."

"I don't know what to do," he muttered again. But he sat and leaned against the side of the tub, sinking to his shoulders under the bubbles.

I left him there, my own anger making it hard to watch his pain. He'd done nothing but express a healthy desire to learn more about himself and his desires and been caught in a trap that had nothing to do with him. The fact that this Kane person had figured out just exactly how to get to me, did nothing for my own nerves. How could anyone know me that well and I have no idea who he fucking was?

I wanted him caught. I wanted him safely behind bars.

I ended up in the kitchen ten minutes later lost in thought, wondering if I would be able to confront the animal and not kill him, when my cell rang. One glance at the display told me it was trouble. Adam never called me on my work cell unless there was something he thought the police needed outside help on.

"Shit." I hit the ON button and put the phone to my ear.

"Need you down here, Gabby. Now. You need to see this and before the CSI runs amok over it."

"What, Adam?"

"Get here." He gave me the address, a gay fetish club outside the Alley with a less than stellar reputation. I committed it to memory and hung up.

I couldn't leave Rory alone. Kane knew where he was. I couldn't take him with me. He was shaken enough, and whatever it was that had Adam so freaked out would not be anything Rory needed to deal with.

Rolly and Marky had a long-standing and firm "do not disturb" order that started every Saturday after the club closed and ended Monday morning when Marky left for his job as Dean's groundskeeper. The one time I'd broken that law, they'd both been so pissed at me, it had taken months to repair the damage to our relationship, both personal and professional. I should have known better anyway. One did not come between a Dom and his sub, ever.

With a heavy sigh and a fervent hope he wasn't completely done with me, I dialled Jimmy's number. Apparently, Adam had filled him in on the details of Rory's encounter with Kane that day, and he agreed to come over and stay with him.

"For his sake, Gabe."

"Thank you."

"Yeah."

He hung up.

Rory wasn't pleased about being hauled out of the tub and told to stay in my room. Nor was he happy about my news that Jimmy would be here to babysit him. I wasn't pleased about leaving him alone knowing Kane knew exactly where he was. I had to have faith in them both to be sensible, though. Adam's demand that I get to the bar immediately had me rattled.

"Let me come with you."

"No."

He watched with deep, black eyes as I strapped my holster in place and checked my gun. I hated the look in his eyes, the way he crawled back against the headboard and curled his arms around his knees, which he'd raised to his chin.

"What happened, Gabe?"

"I don't know, Rory. Adam called me. He didn't say why. I have to go and find out." I slipped a jacket over the gun and sat on the bed. "And you have to stay here. Where it's safe."

"I don't want to be safe. I want it to be over."

"So do I. Trust me. I'm going to find out what's going on and I'll be back. I promise."

"Let me come with you."

"No."

He curled further in on himself when I reached to touch him.

"Not with a gun on," he whispered. "I hate them."

"I'll leave it at the door when I get home. Try and get some rest."

He nodded but didn't look up when I left.

Jimmy

Damn Gabe to hell. It didn't matter that none of this was his fault. I didn't want to be in that house, or around Rory. Not that I had anything against the little shit, personally. He'd only taken my last hope of connecting with the last person I could think of who understood anything about me.

"Fucker."

I skidded my bike into the drive, and Gabe was out the door before I had removed the keys from the ignition.

"Jimmy—"

"Go."

"I—"

"Fuck off." I took the keys he offered and went inside. I didn't give a flying fuck if my attitude pissed him off.

Once inside, I locked the doors and checked the windows. Rory didn't make an appearance, though he mumbled something from the other side of the door to Gabe's bedroom when I knocked.

"Fine."

I wandered to the living room and turned on the TV.

"I haven't babysat since I was fifteen!" I shouted.

No response. I watched TV for a while. Some silly sitcom that made sense only if you smoked enough pot. One did not smoke pot in Gabriel Stark's house. I watched right to the end, but no. It wasn't any better knowing the outcome.

"Like my fucking life," I mumbled, flipping through the channels. "Babysitting is as boring now as it was then!"

"Were you as big a prick then as you are now?" Rory's voice was quiet.

I turned to find him leaning in the doorway. His hair was pulled back with something shiny, and his face was drawn, tired-looking and worried. He'd wrapped his arms around his middle, fingers digging tight into his sides.

"Yes."

He stood there a long while, watching me, and I suddenly felt like a complete jerk. Because a situation was shitty did not give me the right to act like a complete ass. I opened my mouth to apologise, but he turned abruptly and headed down the hallway.

"I'll be in the study. I have to send a few emails."

"Whatever."

I heard him go in and sit at the desktop computer. I wondered if Gabe had given him the password for it, or left it on for him. He'd never given it to me. Not that that ever stopped me. Maybe I *was* a jerk.

Rory

I sat on the couch across from the desk for a few minutes, eyeing the desktop computer. I was fairly certain it would be password protected. I didn't really want to send any emails. I had just hoped coming in here would ease some tension, give me the feeling I was near Gabe somehow. But it was an entirely professional space, and all it did was bring back the image of him getting ready to leave me here.

The sight of him strapping on that gun frightened me all over again. Memories long preceding Kane made thinking straight hard. I had put all those old disasters away a long time ago. Not even Kane's abuse had brought it back the way seeing Gabe with a gun in his hand had. It was foolish. I knew it was. But it didn't stop the realisation that the last time I'd seen that particular scenario, it had ended with me in a hospital bed with my jaw wired shut.

The last person who had promised to protect me hadn't. Maybe it had been a long time ago, but I'd learned the lesson well. Didn't matter that every kid believed that promise from their own father. It apparently didn't apply to a cop's son if that son wasn't going to let himself get beaten straight. At least he hadn't shot me, which, at the time, I had hoped for. It would have been so much easier.

Seemed any time I let people promise to protect me, let myself believe they would, I ended up watching it all fall to shit.

Not this time.

Tiptoeing, and feeling completely idiotic, I peeked out the office door. I heard Jimmy's questionable taste in television muttering from down the hall and crept back to the desk.

A picture of Gina sat on the left corner, along with one of Adam and Peter, one of Jimmy, and another, set off to the side, of a young man I'd never met. His dark hair and eyes and pale skin practically jumped out of the frame at me.

I didn't exactly look like him. My face was longer, thinner, my nose less of a ski jump. I didn't have freckles, and my lips weren't so thin and tight at the corners. I wondered if the man in the photo had forgotten how to laugh. He didn't look much like he enjoyed life.

"Who are you?"

He stared back from behind the glass, no answer, no light in his eyes. He just looked sad.

I set the picture face down on the desk and turned to the window, hoping to ease the sudden cloying feeling of being in someone else's skin, someone else's story. I couldn't stay. Whoever the guy in the photo was, I wasn't going to become him. I couldn't live like that.

I unlocked the French doors of the den, breathed in the fresh night air, stepped out, and tried to imagine myself anywhere but alone in a stranger's house.

Night sounds floated up around me—crickets and the evening breeze, carrying the soft susurration of leaves and grasses in Gabe's garden. The clean smell of turned earth and growing things eventually lured me into the backyard. There wasn't anything to fear in the warm, gently lit garden but a few earthworms and snails. With me settled in the lounge under the trellis, it was almost like the old memories of anger and derision could be shoved back into the dark corners where they belonged.

That man wasn't me. I wasn't him. Gabe would be back soon, and I could ask him. Above all, I knew, as I sat there and gazed around this growing patch of his domain, that this was where I belonged. The past, neither mine nor his, was not going to break us.

Jimmy

Heaving a sigh, I got up and tried not to sulk down the hall. The study door was open. I went in. No Rory.

"What the fuck?"

In the centre of Gabe's desk was a framed photo turned facedown.

"Ten bucks says I know who that's of." I picked it up. Collin.

"Rory?" I called through the house, but got no response. When I went back to the den, I noticed the French doors leading to the garden were open.

"Shit." The light curtains blew in the evening breeze. I could smell the garden coming in the room and hurried over. "Rory!"

Gabe was going to kill me. If anything happened to him...

"I'm right here." His reply came dull and sad out the darkness, and I couldn't help heave a sigh of relief.

"What are you doing?"

"Sitting." After a minute and a soft shuffle, "Thinking."

"About?"

He didn't say anything.

"The picture is of a man named Collin," I told him.

"Where is he now?"

It was odd talking to the dark, but Rory's voice sounded tight. Thick. I let him remain hidden by the shadows. "He died."

"He's the one Gabe couldn't fix."

"It's a long story, Rory."

"And you don't want to tell it?"

I jumped. This new voice came from the opposite end of the yard, smooth, hard, like diamonds glittering in the night.

Rory made a small sound. The chair he was sitting in creaked.

"Rory. Come here." I held out a hand in the direction his voice had come from. "Hurry!"

"Stay where you are." The stranger's voice floated across the yard, closer now, and almost bored sounding, like he had no doubt he would be obeyed.

"Rory!"

I moved towards him. The door slammed behind me, and I cursed, mentally picturing Gabe's house keys sitting in a tangle on his coffee table with mine. Something cold and hard thumped against my leg, just below the hem of my shorts. It was a second before I realised there was pain, and another before the cold, jabbing touch came again and I fell.

I couldn't get up. The backs of my legs stung like hell. I couldn't get my feet under me. I could feel blood and reached around to find it flowing freely from both legs. Once, on the football field, I'd turned too sharp, too quick and fucked up a hamstring. I knew I was in trouble.

"Rory! Run!"

There was only the sound of muffled struggling. The fucker had never even shown his shadow, never mind his face, but I knew the voice.

"Darnel!" I shouted. "Leave him alone. He isn't anything to do with this! Just—"

A boot connected with my temple.

Beyond the buzzing in my ears and the stars and spots frittering my eyesight away, I thought I heard the distinctive squeak of Gabe's garage door. Lights flashed somewhere to my left and went out. The spots grew, the buzzing intensified, and the agony of damaged muscles won.

At least Gabe was saved the bother of killing me himself.

Chapter Ten

Rory

I had seen Jimmy enter the office, look at the picture. I even saw the panic on his face, and I should have called to him or gone back inside. I sat there, not quite ready to deal with his snark and his anger. He had a right to feel it. I just didn't want to face it and know I was taking something he'd hoped would be his someday. Finally, when he came back and stood in the doorway, fear clearly etched on his face, I had spoken up.

I knew Jimmy had recognised the other voice the way his eyes went wide. Kane at last had an identity someone knew, and I started to get up. If Jimmy would just go back inside, call Gabe… I might not make it back in before Kane materialised out of the darkness, but Jimmy was right there by the door.

Instead, Jimmy had come outside. For me. Kane taunted him out, and I saw the sweep of shadow too late. In seconds, Jimmy was sprawled on the ground and Kane was on me.

An arm whipped around my chest and a hand covered my mouth. Too late to shout, too weak to fight my way free. I tried an elbow, tried to open my mouth enough to sink my teeth into that meaty palm.

"Oh, you've grown some balls since last we had a chance to play. That's just going to make this all the sweeter. Take a good look, Rory. Last you'll see of this place, I promise you that. And that picture you were starin' at?"

My captor swung me around to face him. I didn't need to see his face to know it was Kane. "Gabe, the fucker. He killed him. Stupid shit was supposed to be my mate, my best friend. He was supposed to protect him. Instead? You know what he did? He got too close. He fell in love. With *my boyfriend!* And he let him die instead of letting him come home to me."

"Home to a maniac? You hurt people." I pulled in a deep breath and yelled. He cuffed me, bullying pain across my jaw and sending me sprawling. I scrambled away, practically on hands and knees, towards Jimmy. I didn't get far.

"Oh." He grabbed a fist full of my hair and yanked my head back. "I'll hurt you. Don't kid yourself. He loves you, right? You think he does? You're a reflection. A replacement for Collin, and he couldn't keep him, either. Collin would have rather died than stay with him. You will too, before I'm done with you."

There was no time to panic. No time to struggle more. Just blinding pain cracking across my temple and...nothing.

Cuffs were the first thing I recognised. Wrists and ankles shackled and drawn out spread-eagled, and a collar around my neck. The room was dark and silent. It was cold. The floor chilled my bare feet, and I realised I was naked. I had no idea where I was. No one else did, either. No one would even know I was gone until Gabe returned from the call he'd taken that had lured him out of the house. Away from me.

"What did you do?" I knew he was there somewhere, lurking in the dark where I couldn't see him. "Where's Gabe?"

"Safely on the other side of the city by now. Figuring out what's going on, no doubt. But it won't matter. By the time he finds you, there won't be anything left. You escaped once. Don't think it will happen again." His hand splayed over my back, between my shoulder blades. "You pissed me off, Rory. I don't like being pissed off."

He pushed down. The collar, snug around my throat, was tied off somewhere. It ground into my throat, cut off my air. Choking was going to be a horrible way to die.

I'd been wrong to think Kane's vendetta had nothing to do with me. If it hadn't to begin with, it did now. I'd escaped his clutches, found Gabe and found hope. He was not going to let me keep any of it. I shouldn't have been surprised when the bite of the lash fell across my back. This wasn't under the guise of training anymore. He didn't have to be careful enough to keep me whole. I wasn't brave or strong enough to do anything but hope I didn't last long.

Gabe

I knew the minute I arrived at the club and went inside why Adam had called me. There was a pall over the scene that only happened when ugly death was in this building. I knew the moment I laid eyes on Adam's face I didn't want to see what was inside the small room he stood guard outside.

"I'm sorry to put you through this, Gabriel." Those were his first words. And he called me Gabriel.

I stopped outside the closed door. "Then don't."

"I need your help with this one. There are things about this you need to see personally, and I'm not going to get away with showing you if you don't get in here before anyone else shows up. Please."

Hating the very idea of looking at a dead body, even for Adam, I let him lead me into the room. There is a stench to the dead you never forget. Once before I'd smelled it, and that memory woke me nights, even years later. This one was going to do the same.

Long black hair spread everywhere. Blood that hadn't had time to clot dried on skin that would have been pale even without the pallor of death.

"Eyes are blue," Adam said softly. "But how many lookalikes can there be in one city? Have a look. This is what killed him."

He crouched and peeled away one of the cuffs on the thin wrists. Pink cotton bandages beneath, once pried back, revealed slits along the veins.

"Not self-inflicted. He bled out while these bandages were being applied. This was messy, Gabe. Messy—"

"And personal," I finished for him.

"Who is he?"

"Fucked if I know!" I hadn't meant to shout, but the hard truth, that I was to blame for this tragedy for some unknown reason, was staring up at me from dead eyes.

"Someone who knew Collin. Knew what happened to him."

"The only people who knew about his first attempt were you, Peter, me and Jimmy. As far as anyone else knew, the overdose was how he died. He didn't want anyone to know about him cutting himself. You know that."

"Then he told someone." Adam stood and gazed down at the body.

"He didn't have anyone. Just Darnel, and after that disastrous relationship, I can't imagine he would tell him. Soon as Darnel shipped out, Collin came to me and didn't have contact with him ever after that. Not that I know of."

"Then the maniac had contact with him. Somehow. Think."

I shook my head. "He never came around our place. Collin spent all his time at the house. Mostly in the garage working on that car."

"Collin was never free of him. Somehow, he had contact with him. Somehow, he knew about Collin slitting his wrist, and he knew about the pink bandages. This is about you, Gabe. This maniac killed this guy to send you a message."

"What if I was right?" Frostbitten memories came back, of Collin in his hospital bed, making promises, begging me to take him back, to help him. Warmer ones, ones where he smiled even, after I took him home again pushed those out. "What if Collin was getting better, and the overdose was not self-administered? If Darnel did have contact with Collin, and Collin told him to fuck off, what Kane said to Rory in the mall would make more sense. If Kane is Darnel, and now I can't imagine he's not…" I let out a healthy string of curses. How had I missed it? How had I not known? Darnel had been my best friend at one time. I hadn't ever felt comfortable about him joining the army after high school, and combat had done some horrific damage to him. We tried to mend him, Peter and I, and at one point, I even thought Collin might have been good for him. I never once suspected how very bad Darnel had been for poor Collin.

"Everything is so fucking obvious when you know the answer," I muttered.

In the periphery of my awareness, Adam's radio crackled to life. He said something, and a static response came, gibberish to my ears as I stared at the corpse. A man who had died solely to prove to me that Kane could get into the very heart of me and rip it out.

"I have to get home."

"Gabe—"

Just the tone of Adam's voice sent ice and fear through me. I lifted my gaze at last, to confirm what Adam hadn't said. "This was a fucking distraction!"

"I sent a uniform around to check on them. He found Jimmy—" His eyes watered, but he blinked that news away. "The ambulance just arrived."

"Rory?"

He shook his head. "But we'll find him, Gabe."

"Fuck. No, you won't. Not before he's dead. Tortured and dead."

It didn't matter. I didn't need them. I knew now who had done it all. I knew what he wanted. And I knew exactly where I'd find him.

"Gabe!"

Adam came crashing after me, shouting over his shoulder at someone to secure something. I didn't care. I'd seen what my old, dead friend Darnel wanted me to see. I'd done exactly what his new incarnation, Kane, wanted me to do. I was walking, running, in fact, into a trap. I'd probably find Rory, caught, hooked, bait. The odds of him even being alive by the time I reached him were slim, although I wouldn't put it past Kane to keep him hovering, just to let me see the damage, see the pain and fear, and watch the light go.

Speed limit be damned, I couldn't make the car go fast enough, couldn't get around the pedestrians and the slower traffic, couldn't run enough red lights. Couldn't get there fast enough. There may or may not have been sirens battering the night aside behind me. It didn't matter. Nothing mattered if I lost again.

Rory

Long after I lost count of the lashes and stopped actually feeling the pain, the whip kept falling. I closed my eyes against the light. It was bright, biting into my head, making it hard to think. I'd already seen enough to know Kane hadn't even taken me far. I had seen Gabe's backyard through a long, narrow window and tangle of overgrown raspberry plants, when I'd been able to stand upright. Now, I was on my knees on the cold cement. Nearby, a lumpy car hidden under a white cover and a tool chest, sparkling like only tool chests that had barely been used could, told me I had to be in a garage. Probably Gabe's. So close, and yet, there was no reason for him to look here.

Idly, I watched a trickle of blood meander across the cement under my knees. I wondered how much a person had to bleed to have enough of the stuff on the outside that it could run in little rivulets like that. It seemed a very disconnected thought to be having, considering that blood was my own, from wounds ripped open by the devil's tail Kane was still using on me. It occurred to me I probably had very little skin left on my back. It didn't seem to matter.

When the collar around my neck began to dig into my skin, that mattered a bit. I was losing the ability to hold myself up. At some point, the collar was going to be the only thing keeping me off the cold cement.

How long did it take to choke to death?

"Not yet, precious."

Kane came around in front. I saw the toes of his boots. I'd seen that view so many times. To think once I'd wanted so badly to please him, I would have licked those boots if he'd demanded it. Now, I spat on them.

He kicked me, hard in the shoulder, and it gave with an oddly loud pop. The collar dug into my throat. I probably screamed. It seems likely that would be a proper response, but it was hard to breathe, so maybe not.

"Uh-uh, sweetheart. You don't get to check out until Gabe gets here. You get to watch him watch you die." Fingers dug into my hair, pulled my head up, taking the pressure off the collar. "You should have just gone home after that night at Rolly's. Let me clean you up, make you mine. You wouldn't have had to die."

"Fuck you."

"No, you're the one who gets fucked, and dear old Gabe can watch that, too. He can hear you tell him how you don't want him. That you belong to me. Do that and I won't kill him too." He gave my head another yank and I couldn't help but whimper. "Tell him you would rather die than ever let him touch you again."

"Is that what Collin said to you?"

"I couldn't let him have him, could I?" For a moment, just on the edge of Kane's rock hard tone, was something else. Almost, someone else. Someone very sad and lonely. "He wouldn't come back to me. I guess...maybe... He wouldn't come back, so I had to take him." His voice went whispery thin. "I didn't really mean to hurt him. He wasn't supposed to die. I just wanted…"

"You wanted him to love you."

He nodded. "I just…missed him. But he wanted Gabe and I didn't know what to do. I snapped."

Fuck, I did not want to have sympathy for this man! I curled a lip against my own softness. "So killing him would definitely be better than letting him go."

I fully expected the hard slap and the pressure that jammed my throat into the collar again. But he didn't even let me lose consciousness. "Gabriel fucking Stark can watch you scream and bleed and beg. He doesn't get you back. He doesn't get you too. I won't let him win again!"

I scrabbled my feet against the slippery floor, pushed against the collar. Maybe if I died before Gabe figured this nightmare out, I could spare him watching this animal torture me. I wasn't about to let this freak use my suffering to hurt Gabe.

"Don't bother. You don't have any control here. You're the slave. I'm the Master."

He lifted me, propped me up until he could tighten my arms and hold me erect. Pain sheered through my dislocated shoulder. It was enough to keep me conscious, and I glared at him.

"That's what you think," I informed him. "I'm not afraid of you any more, asshole. You can hurt me, and you'll probably kill me. You'll never own me. I belong to Gabe. Is that why you're so pissed? Because the last poor man you tortured chose him, too? You can't own people through fear. It doesn't work that way."

"Shut up."

"Cut out my tongue."

"Don't tempt me."

"No. I get to keep it so Gabe can hear me beg, right? He won't because he knows everything that matters. He knows I love him. He knows I'm his." Kane didn't have to know that wasn't the complete truth. He didn't have the right to be privy to Gabe's uncertainty, and in my heart, I knew what was true. "Nothing you can do to me matters, because nothing will ever change what we both know. Just like nothing will ever bring back whoever it is you think he killed. Dead is dead. If your man loved you, he loved you even through all the shit you put him through. If he didn't, nothing you do will ever change that."

"You think you're so very tough. Everyone breaks eventually."

I knew he was probably right. He would, eventually, make me beg him to stop. He wouldn't kill me. Not yet, anyway, and if I could stay alive long enough, Gabe would be able to stop this monster hurting anyone else. As long as I was alive, Kane would stay. I had to keep him here long enough for Gabe to find him and stop him hurting anyone else.

He wasn't going to let me die on my own terms, so he sure as shit didn't get to dictate the terms on which I chose to live.

Gabe

I parked the car on the street. If the sirens had ever been following me, I'd left them behind. Jimmy's ambulance had screeched past me going in the opposite direction at the corner. At least he was still alive.

Around the house, darkness and stillness reigned. The street was quiet, just the sounds of crickets and bullfrogs breaking the suburban calm. A cop car sat in the driveway, one door open and spilling light and pinging noises across the front lawn. The officer was talking on his radio. I ignored him, knowing he likely figured he'd checked everywhere. I headed down the side yard to the garage, neglected since Collin's death, hidden behind the growth of raspberries and Virginia creeper.

I didn't bother going in the house. I knew Rory wouldn't be there. I set my sights on the garage and crept along the narrow path between the sumac bushes and the garage. It was hardly perfect cover, but it let me get under the window in the side of the building where I could hear voices issuing from inside. I couldn't even hear the street noises from back here.

Kane's voice, which I recognised now I knew who he was, issued orders, laughed. Rory screamed. On the street on my other side, a car rolled up, silent, dark. Adam had followed me, after all. The car door opened, and in a moment, Adam was beside me.

More shadows moved through the night at the front of the building. My own fucking garage. Fitting. Collin had died there, in the car I'd bought him, OD'd on the pills the hospital had sent home with him. Pills I hadn't bothered to keep safely out of his grasp.

Dark forms swarmed the building. More cops. I needed to hang back and let them do their jobs. Every scream shattered me. I was shaking so bad I could barely hold my gun. I was worse than useless. I was a danger to everyone, but I couldn't sit back and do nothing.

A huge, dark mass of man appeared in front of me. A bear paw descended onto my shoulder. Adam's whispered voice snaked through my sweating, bloated panic.

"Stay."

"Rory—"

"Please, Gabe. Stay."

I nodded. Part of me wanted nothing more than to sink down there in the loam and rotting leaves and cry. Part of me wanted to go in there and kill the fucker.

"Rory needs you alive and out of jail," Adam hissed, reaching to his belt and unclipping things in near silence. "I don't have time to haul your ass back to the car and cuff you there. Stay. Wait. Be here for Rory. He needs you."

He screamed again, and I thought my skin would peel off.

Adam left, then. I tried to follow, only to find he had actually cuffed me, securing my wrist to a nearby tree, and I'd been too distracted by Rory's obvious distress to notice.

Fucker!

But he was already gone into the night, and I was left behind to listen and wait and break apart as Rory suffered.

They were taking too long. Three more times I listened to that terrible sound, to the sobbing in between, to his pain, and cursed every slow, careful step Adam took that didn't get him there fast enough to prevent it.

Rory

Of course, Kane was right. I begged. He found ways to hurt me that I knew weren't going to kill me. They barely even bloodied me up. They might not even leave marks on my corpse. No matter how much I tried to remember what Gabe's hands felt like, his touch, his kisses, Kane wouldn't let me stay in the dream. It was torture for fun. There was no one there to see it. It was for his personal pleasure. He'd slipped from merely sadistic to psychopathic. I wanted out. I wanted Gabe.

I probably begged for him.

I found myself leaning into the collar again, the blackness edging in on my vision, the numbness overcoming me in the only release I could find. Maybe Kane was getting bored. Maybe all the noise and chaos around us was getting too much for him.

I sagged, no longer caring what he did. I was sorry not to see Gabe again, sorry he'd find me like this, but not sorry he wouldn't have to listen to me plead or scream for him. Not sorry about that.

Then, almost like a dream, like some angel out of a dream that couldn't be real, but that I let myself believe, I did feel his hands in the end. His hands easing me into the darkness where nothing mattered but that he knew, finally, in the end of everything, that I belonged to him.

No matter what circumstances brought me to him, I was, in my heart, his.

Epilogue

One Year Later – Rory

Some days, there were not enough painkillers in the world. Some days, there were only scars and darkness, and some nights, only nightmares. Sometimes, I wished Kane had killed me.

Every day, I struggled to find the man Gabriel Stark had fallen in love with. He kept telling me I was there. Somewhere, buried under the terror and the pain, I was there. It felt like eons before I found a glimmer of myself again. It was maybe a year. Six months after the last surgery to fix my knees, but a year can be a long time when every day hurts and every night is terrifying.

Every day, he watched me. He'd taken my house key away. No knives or drugs he didn't administer with his own hand. No shaving myself or bathing alone. No autonomy of any kind. I didn't want it. I was lost when he wasn't by my side. In the end, Kane broke me, gave Gabe a dead, hollowed-out husk. He'd paid for it with his own life. I had a vague memory of shouting and gunshots. Even vague was too vivid.

"Make it go away."

"I can't, love." Gabe's hand smoothed over my hair. "You have to decide when it stops. I can't do that for you."

I snuggled closer to him, curling beside him on the bed, half starved, still, aching and chilly, even though summer-evening sun streamed through the wide open windows and warmed the room.

I could only think of one way to make it stop, and he'd refused me that out. "Why do you make me stay?"

I knew he knew what I meant. That I wanted to die, and I knew he hated to hear that kind of talk. But he never shushed me, never refused to let me say it.

"It will get easier."

I sighed. "He made me into Collin. Your Collin, who you couldn't save. That's all he wanted in the first place. He won."

"No." Gabe kissed the top of my head. "You are not Collin." He shifted, pushed me to sitting, and cupped my face. "You remember when I said a man who wants to die will find a way?"

I nodded.

"A man who really wants to die will find a way, yet here you are. Still with me. Why?"

I didn't have an answer for him. I'd never thought about why I hadn't yet done what I so often thought I wanted to.

He moved his hand, and one thumb smoothed over my forehead. He drew me close and placed a kiss there. "Get undressed and come to bed."

"It's too early."

"Do as you're told, Rory."

"Yes, Sir."

Once I had settled beside him, he leaned on one elbow, facing me and gazing down at me. "You will get through this, Rory."

"What makes you so sure?"

His fingers worked through the tangles of curls at my temple, stroked over my face, touched my lips. His smile warmed my heart. "You're alive. You're here." He brushed his lips over my forehead. "I want you to understand this, love. You were never a replacement for Collin. I cared very much about him. I knew he was damaged. I knew I probably would never be able to fix him, not the way he needed. I hoped I could give him something, like the strength to go on long enough to find his own healing. I was wrong and foolish to think I could give him what he couldn't find in himself."

"How am I different? Since I came home, you haven't let me out of your sight. It's like a death watch."

"Collin gave himself up to Kane long before I ever met him. If he ever tried to break free, it wasn't because of me. It never had anything to do with me. Kane owned him so completely he couldn't live with it. It wasn't being submissive he hated. It wasn't even Kane. It was losing himself that he couldn't live with. When I look into your eyes, I *know* you're in there. I know you know it. Whatever it is you're holding onto, it's important enough to keep you here. Keep you alive. It isn't anything I did. It's what's inside you that matters so much to you."

"I want to make you proud of me."

"I already am. This isn't about me. It's about that piece of you I know is still alive in there."

"You keep saying that."

When he leant down for a kiss, it occurred to me in the months since I'd come back to his house, he hadn't touched me or tried to kiss me. He'd made it clear he was available if I wanted, but he'd never made a move himself. That first kiss — short, tender, barely a brush of warm, dry lips over mine — sent me reeling.

I blinked up at him, my breath pumping in short, sharp gasps. His fingers resumed their exploration of my face. His gaze remained steady on mine. It wasn't the first time since I'd physically recovered that I felt the surge of want riding my bloodstream. It was the first time I raised the nerve to do anything about it.

And all I managed was to lift a hand and touch his cheek. He moved his head, if not his gaze, and kissed my palm. "I'm still alive," I whispered.

His smile did more to warm me than the quilt or the sun or the hot summer breeze flowing in the windows.

"You are."

"It's over."

"It is."

"I don't...hate what I am."

He tilted his head slightly. "You hesitate?"

"No. Not really. I stayed alive because I knew there was one thing he could never touch."

"What?"

"Us. That in the deepest part of me, I'm yours, and that's okay." I shifted up onto an elbow, coming even with him. "Death watch is over. I'm not going to kill myself. I'll still have nightmares and bad days. Kane wanted to turn me into some pathetic creature you couldn't have. All he did was teach me who I was all along, and show me I have the power to chose who I belong to."

Gabe levelled a stern look at me. "If you say 'I chose you' I might puke."

I actually laughed, a small, relieved chuckle, to know we could be human about it all.

He smiled and touched my face, like he was learning it for the first time.

"But I don't. I chose me."

I knew the frown would come, and the hurt. I took his hand and kissed his knuckles. "That's what you've been trying to show me all along, isn't it? That I can't give myself to anyone unless I own myself and who I am first. So, here I am. The slightly dinged-up floor model of me with a violent past, a hateful father, and a bucket of angst. Scratch and dent sale. You want?"

This time, Gabe's kiss was pure possession. His weight toppling me onto my back and his hands cupping my face, roving down my body, were everything I wanted. He was passionate and careful, possessive and accommodating, opening me up to all the possibilities, even the ones I'd once told him were absolute hard limits.

I might never be fit for restraints or whips again, but when his fingers caressed over my hole and he drew back, a question in his eyes, I nodded. I trusted him to take what I'd given him and treat it with care.

And he did. I'd been in and out of hospitals enough over the past year to know I was healthy and well on my way to full recovery, physically.

I'd been right about the condom being HIV positive, though it hadn't been Kane's DNA in it, and I had been given a clean bill. They were still trying to figure out whose it was, though I thought it probably didn't matter. Since Kane had died, fetish clubs throughout the city had adopted quite a few stricter rules and regulations. Rolly was probably behind the new entrance requirements though, as always, he never seemed to leave his tower except to go home and disappear into his castle with Marky.

"What are you thinking about?"

I shook my head. "Nothing important."

I shifted under him, well aware of my limitations. Kane had done a lot of physical damage. I'd never be physically strong again. Smashed knee caps and broken bones just didn't always heal as strong as they'd been.

Gabe rolled me onto my side, curled himself around my back, and proceeded to probe my ass and kiss along my neck, giving me pleasure and attention in ways I'd forgotten were possible.

"Okay?" he whispered, licking along my earlobe.

I nodded. I could feel the tingling skin of my scars pressed against his hairy chest, and gasped when his fingers strayed over the line of marked skin where the collar Kane had used had cut deep into the skin over my clavicle.

He didn't draw away, but caressed the scar until I shivered.

"Don't."

"Shh." He didn't move his hand. Below, his fingers still pumped methodically in and out of my ass. The hand on my neck smoothed over the scar again.

"Gabe, please stop."

His hand stilled, but when I didn't use my safe word, he rolled me over onto my back, looked into my eyes for a moment. I couldn't look away. I didn't know what to say. Finally, he bent and kissed the scar, running his tongue over the blight.

My breath hissed out between my teeth at the tingling not-pain, not-pleasure of the sensation. I squirmed to get my chin in his way, but his gentle hand lifted it again.

"Shh. Lie still." He had the edge of command in his voice. The implacable strength that told me he wasn't going to back down on this.

I stilled.

"Every part of you is lovely to me, Rory."

"His marks—"

"Are part of you, and you said you belong to me. That makes them mine, too, and I'll touch them if I want."

"Yes, Sir." I silently cursed myself for trembling every time his fingers found another bit of discoloured, contorted skin.

"Do you think you're ugly?"

How could he ask that? Scratched and dented didn't begin to describe what Kane had done to my body. It was far from the pristine, milky smooth skin I'd had when Gabe met me, marked though it had been then. Those marks would have faded, eventually. Between the scars from the lash and the collar and from the surgeries, I was hardly the picture of beauty.

His fingers moved on my collarbone. Evidently, I'd taken too long to answer. He rubbed at the scar again, and I shivered. His fingers slid back inside me, but didn't otherwise move.

"Answer the question. I know you don't use my bath anymore. You don't like the mirrors."

"Will you take them down?"

"No."

"I don't like the way I look." I closed my eyes, turned my head so he couldn't see my face.

"Do you think if there was no physical sign, it would be easier to forget?" he asked. His lips found my jaw, my cheek bone, nibbled at my ear.

"No."

"So those marks. Those are his."

"No."

"No. They aren't. Why?"

I took a deep breath, managed to stop the shrill spread of panic and anger. "Because they are part of me, and nothing of me belongs to him. I belong to myself, and all I am, I've given to you."

He withdrew his hand from my ass, wrapped it around my hip, and pulled me close against his groin. "Mine," he confirmed in a low growl that vibrated against the skin of my neck where his lips touched.

I rolled slightly, pressed my ass against his hard cock. My trust in Gabe's care warred with my memories of the pain Kane had visited on me this way. But what was a bad memory, if not just another scar? And I'd given myself, scars and all, into the hands of this man who held me now. It was his right to touch them if he cared to, and mine to accept his touch.

He was slow and methodical about taking me, big hands prying, cock stretching me wide open, filling me. It was too much, and still not enough. I wasn't hard anymore by the time he was fully seated, but still I panted and shivered, tried to keep the whimpers and sniffling to a silent minimum.

His arms were steel bands around my chest, his big hands clamps around my wrists. I huddled in that tight cocoon, shaking and completely at his mercy.

"What's your safeword, Rory?"

"I don't need it." I pressed back against him, needing the reassurance of his warmth.

"Tell me what it is."

"Yaoimagic," I whispered, praying he wouldn't pull out. I'd come this far. I wanted to at least give him the chance to find his own release.

"Good."

His breath floated along my neck, and a moment later, I felt his nose nudge in behind my ear. Sometimes, he slept that way, his face buried in my hair. I had no idea how he breathed like that, but it was nice having the sound of his breath so close.

When he started moving it was slow, sweet, barely a movement at all. Gradually, his thrusts increased, his panting, and the pressure of his body all around tightening to match. Then he hit my gland and my animal cry echoed around the room. I arched, and his rhythm soon had us both, and the bed, rocking. He let go of one wrist and his big hand went down to cover my cock and balls, playing until he coaxed my excitement back to life.

I came hard and messily all over his fingers and the bed, and he followed only seconds behind.

It was very unmanly of me to sob the way I did. Right up there with the pretty hair clips. Still. He didn't seem to mind that I cried myself to sleep against his chest.

Gabe

I knew Rory's emotional release would far outdo his physical one. I was surprised he got off on the act at all, though it pleased me he managed to relax enough to enjoy it. Some small part of me had begun to worry this breakthrough might never come, and that, indeed, Kane had won.

But he was strong. Strong enough to let me see his tears. I hid mine behind his anguish and just held him. I managed to get myself back under control by the time he wound down and slept.

He was a different person in the morning. I'd thought his announcement the night before that he was turning the corner might be the start of something. I couldn't have imagined the turnaround in my wildest, brightest dreams.

I'd left him sleeping when I went to my office and came out to find our bed cleaned and him making breakfast.

"I hope you're hungry," he enthused.

He had his hair up in a band on top of his head. It was nice to see it finally pulled away from his face, but I wondered why a plain, boring headband.

"What?" He glanced up from the scrambled eggs. "You're staring."

"You're going to eat scrambled eggs and toast?"

"I know." His hand flitted over his belly. He was skin and bones. So painfully thin I sometimes worried I'd hurt him if I hugged him too hard. "I don't remember the last time I actually woke up hungry. Great, isn't it?"

I nodded. Beyond great. And far beyond that because he knew he was in trouble, and he recognised the need to do something about it, at last.

I watched him dump eggs onto a plate and arrange toast. He hadn't lost his flair for a pretty plate even if he had been absent from the kitchen a long time. The hot food was plain but good. Probably better he hadn't made it anything fancy. It would take time to get him back on a regular diet.

"I have to ask you something." He'd eaten about half his meal and was slowly whittling away at the rest.

"Ask."

Three false starts later, all he said was, "Tell me the story."

And after everything he'd suffered, I didn't have the right to refuse him that.

So I told him about Peter, myself and Darnel, how we'd grown up together, all the shit and the good times that happen in high school. Then Peter went off to college, Darnel the military. I stayed. I made a life in Rainbow Alley and introduced Adam to Peter when he was home on Christmas vacation. I tried hard to understand the ways active combat had changed Darnel when he got his discharge.

"I guess," Rory poked his eggs round his plate, "war changes people. My mom said the same thing. That Dad wasn't the same when he came home. Doesn't make it okay. Maybe just explains."

"Maybe. But he hurt people. Even people he professed to love. He claimed he loved Collin, and yet, Collin came to me so hurt there was nothing I could do for him except offer him safety. And I was pretty shit at that. For both of you."

"Here's the thing." Rory set down his fork and leaned across the table. "First off, someone who wants something bad enough will get it. One way or another. Kane—Darnel—was hurt. He wanted to hurt you back, and he did. He wanted to break me, and he did. And don't say he didn't. I'm patched back together, but I'm not the man I was. There's nothing wrong with who I am, but he changed me. So what? Second, you did everything in your power to keep me safe. If I'd listened and kept my ass in the house like you said, he wouldn't have caught me. That was my fault, not yours, and not Jimmy's."

A cloud passed over his face. I think part of his despair all this time had a lot to do with Jimmy. He'd had to watch Kane cut him down, and not be able to help or go to him. He'd made himself watch Jimmy's painful recovery, though the two men had yet to speak to each other, and right from day one, Adam and Peter had kept me away from him. They were furious that I'd gotten him involved at all.

I didn't blame them one bit. I was furious with myself on that point. Once again, I'd fucked up, and Jimmy had paid for it. I'd taken advantage of his inability to say no to me and there was nothing I could do to make that up to him.

"He made his choice," Rory said quietly, his dark eyes never leaving my face.

I didn't know if he meant Jimmy or Collin. Or both.

"I just wish I knew why Collin needed out so badly," I admitted. I mean, the first time, I got that. He told me how much he hated what he'd become under Darnel. How he didn't think he could ever be sane again. But I thought…I really thought he was getting there. Starting to, anyway. I never expected him to try again."

"He didn't."

"What?" I'd been pushing the food around my own plate, staring at the mangled mess of toast crumbs and eggs. Now I looked up to find Rory still watching me, eyes wide, face pale. "Rory? What?"

"Something K–Darnel said. In the garage. He said, 'I couldn't let him' — meaning you — 'have him. He left me, so I took him back. Like I will you.' Then, later, he said he didn't mean it. He didn't mean for him to die. When Collin told him he was never going back, that he wanted you, he snapped. That's how he put it. That he snapped."

"You make it sound like Darnel gave Collin the drugs that killed him."

"I think maybe he did. Or he thought he did." He shook his head. "I don't know. I guess now we'll never know for sure." He picked up his fork and speared the last of his eggs. "For what it's worth, I'm sorry you lost them both. I'm sorry that happened to Darnel."

I couldn't help a small chuckle. "You should hate him."

"And where did hating you get him? A cop bullet in his head and an early grave. How many men did he hurt? Hate doesn't really get you anywhere, does it?"

"No."

There was nothing simple or ordinary about the man sitting across from me, and from what I could see, what I knew, there was nothing but beauty in him, even after, and maybe because of what he'd endured.

"Come here." I stood and held out my hand. "I've been wanting to give you something since you came home. The time never really seemed right."

He took my hand and followed, docile, to the couch where he waited while I went to the den and brought back a gift I'd bought. I'd meant it as a coming home gift, but it hadn't been appropriate at the time.

"What is it?" He took the box, flipped it open. "Hey." He picked up the shimmering hair clip from its black velvet nest. "This is the very first one you bought me."

"It is. I wanted to give it to you when you came home from the hospital, but—"

"No hair." He smiled sadly. "I still don't know why they had to shave it *all* off. It was a little cut."

"It was one hundred and three stitches and a cracked skull."

"Whatever." He swept the nondescript band out of his hair and stood so he could see his reflection in the mirror above the fireplace.

I watched him adorn the short fall of curls with the cheap bauble. Watched the smile seep into his eyes and flush his cheeks as he turned his head to admire himself.

"Fuck, that is hot," I muttered.

"You make no sense," Rory told me as he came back to the couch and settled in my lap.

"I can't explain it. It just makes me want to…well… We should go upstairs."

"And mess up the sheets I just put on the bed?"

"Yes."

He leaned close, eyes sparkling, licked his lips, and touched them to mine. I couldn't resist. The man knew how to take a kiss from me, and how to give it back tenfold.

When he finally let me go, he smiled.

"Okay."

About the Author

Jaime writes, romance, fantasy, urban fantasy, shifter stories about men, about life, about love. Her work is populated with mostly men, most of whom are into each other, and yes, we do mean into each other. You can find plenty of free reading on her website.

She also reviews for Dark Diva Reviews, mostly the same types of stories, and will happily spout her opinion on the books she reads to her kids, who she home schools. Finally, she's occasionally gainfully employed. She writes for the love it, and hopes to pass on that love to her readers, her kids, and anyone else who comes along.

Jaime Samms loves to hear from readers. You can find her contact information, website details and author profile page at http://www.total-e-bound.com.

Total-E-Bound Publishing

www.total-e-bound.com

Take a look at our exciting range of literagasmic™
erotic romance titles and discover pure quality
at Total-E-Bound.

.